A SONG *and a* SNOWFLAKE

ALIVIA FLEUR

SPENCER & CO
PUBLISHING

A prequel could only be for David.
Because everything began with you.

Welcome to Honeysuckle Street

In a quiet corner of London, on the north side of the river, is a little street called Honeysuckle Street.

Don't bother looking for it now—you won't find it on any map. But once, before progress was the catchword of the day, Honeysuckle Street cut a treelined path between two main thoroughfares. The street itself could comfortably accommodate two carriages passing by one another. The residents spent their days in each other's company, or spotted one another on walks, or attended balls and gatherings together. A few errant children played games, and the odd elderly neighbour watched from behind twitching curtains, muttering about *young people these days*.

An enterprising developer had purchased the entire row on the north side of the street, cleared it and erected in its place five terrace townhouses. Five stories high, modelled on the Belgrave style and as similar on the outside as they were on the inside, which is to say, apart from the inhabitants, they were identical.

Five villas, each four or five stories high lined the opposite side of the street, mostly built at some stage during the reigns of the past kings named George.

And king of it all was a grey cat with a white-tipped tail named Spencer.

Spencer lived at number 6, the house in the middle of the street on the south side. It was rumoured that the old lady who occupied the house had been a lover of the Russian Tsar. Others said she had made and lost several fortunes in the American West. Others said that she had scrimped every penny she earned as a washerwoman and made a sensible investment during the last financial downturn. No one knew for sure. She didn't receive callers. She didn't make house calls.

She passed her time in the company of her beloved cats. At the end of each day, she stood on the porch and called them in. 'Mittens! Georgiana! Jimmy! Spencer! And no matter if they were curled up in the last ray of sun, or stalking along a limb, the little cats would run at the sound of her voice.

All except Spencer.

When he didn't return home, the old lady would wander the streets, calling and calling, 'Spencer! Spencer! Time for tea!' Later, when her hearing faded, she took to banging a pot with a spoon. When it suited him, Spencer would emerge, saunter his way to the house in the middle of the street, where the old lady would scald him but later, when sat by the fire, Spencer was still allowed to curl up and sleep on her lap.

When the old lady died, and unable to locate an heir, the authorities boarded up the old house. The furniture was pilfered. And after applying at kitchen doors, the kittens found new homes.

All except Spencer.

Spencer continued to patrol his street, hunting mice and chasing away noisier, bossier toms who might encroach on his territory. In return, the residents of Honeysuckle Street would find a scrap for him. Miss Delaney's cook left him the joint from the roast on Sunday.

Miss Hartright put out a saucer of cream each night after her aunt had turned in. Mr Babbage put out a slice of cold ham, and not to be outdone, Mr Hempel left out two. The Caplin care-taker snuck him a biscuit, and in the evening, Miss Abberton left the downstairs window ajar so that he could squeeze himself inside and curl up by the furnace, even though he always managed to get by cook and took the best chair in the parlour instead.

Each morning and evening, Spencer sat on the decaying porch of the house in the middle of the street, silently surveying his charges. He kept watch on their comings and goings, their petty feuds and their longing looks over fences. He knew them all, sometimes better than they knew themselves.

Welcome to Honeysuckle Street.

WHO LIVES ON HONEYSUCKLE STREET?

February 1870

Number 1

Phineas Babbage, Bank Clerk

Number 2

Odette Delaney, Soprano

Number 3

Lawrence and Wilhelmina Hempel, Hotel Magnates

and their children:

Rosanna

Johannes

Elliot

Beatrice

Garnett (deceased)

Amadeus

Nova

Number 4

Albert Abberton, Trader and businessman

Iris Abberton, Albert's adopted daughter

Number 5

Mrs Crofts, President of the Society for the Promotion of Civic Morality and the Adherence to Proper Values

Number 6

Dilapidated and abandoned house inhabited by Spencer, King of Honeysuckle Street

Number 7

Petunia Hartright, choir leader

And her visiting nieces

Charlise Hartright

Elise Hartright

Number 8

Dalton earldom town residence, vacant, Dalton family currently residing at their estate

Number 9

Benton Hunter, Diplomat, currently abroad

Number 10

His Grace Arley West, Duke Osborne

CHAPTER ONE

December 18, 1870

'Allow me.'

The baron's white gloved hand intruded into the grey half-light of the carriage. From Charlise's seat, his face remained shadowed, and she hesitated in reaching for him. The day before, she had almost taken a tumble because he hadn't held her firm enough. Or maybe she had not held his hand as tight as she should.

As she gripped the rail to counter her balance, Charlise clasped his hand and gingerly stepped down, her boots clicking as she landed on the granite paved road. She brushed her skirts neat, even though in the dark chill of evening no one would see if her silks were crushed, but the baron always made a comment if she didn't look her best.

The day had already started to fade, and evening crept across the sky. The little group clustered on the path—the baron, who had offered to escort them across town, her sister, Elise, her eyes bright and filled with the sparkles of youthful wonder, and Aunt Petunia, who ascended three steps before she spun to face them and spread her arms wide.

'Welcome to Number 7 Honeysuckle Street,' she said with unabashed pride. 'What do you think?'

Last summer, their aunt had purchased one in an identical stretch of five white stucco-clad townhouses in a quiet part of London. A dedicated bluestocking and proud spinster, the townhouse represented the independence their aunt valued. She had written gushing letters detailing how elegant and modern her new home was—fitted with cast-iron pipes, a kitchen with a hot water boiler that also serviced the bathrooms, and gas lamps in every room. And even though Charlise, her sister, and their father lived only on the opposite side of London, the months had been cluttered with rehearsals and other commitments, and today was their first time visiting for themselves.

Looking along the short strip that was Honeysuckle Street, Charlise could see why her aunt loved it so much. Ancient trees, now stripped of leaves but likely rich and verdant in the summer, dotted the sidewalk. The houses opposite were a quaint, if slightly jumbled looking row of much older homes, a contrast to the modern townhouses. At one end of the street, a towering palatial villa glimmered in the afternoon light, while a warm orange glow emanated in the windows of its neighbour, a slightly smaller earth brown brick home. However, beside it, Number 6 and Number 8 looked completely uninhabited.

'Aunt Petunia,' Charlise called over her shoulder. 'Why are those two houses opposite so dark?'

Her aunt clicked back down a couple of steps to join her on the path. 'No one lives in Number 6. You can't tell now, but it's a terrible shamble. Broken windows, loose boards. Incredibly beautiful in its day, and it would be again if someone had the energy and funds to repair it. But it's too run down for my tastes, despite the attractive price. At my age, I prefer the simplicity of the modern.'

'And its neighbour?' Charlise asked.

'Since the Dalton tragedy seven years ago, the earl has not been to town. I heard that losing his wife and his heir in one day turned him cruel and jaded, although others say he always was. Apart from a caretaker, no one lives there, and probably just as well. My neighbour, Mrs Crofts, says the surviving son was quite a reprobate.'

'Hamish? A reprobate?' A warm, full-bodied peal of laughter came from an self-assured, red-haired woman who seemed to have appeared in their midst as they'd been looking across the street. 'Petunia, you should not listen to gossip, especially that delivered by Mrs Crofts and her society. Hamish crushed her roses once, and she never forgave him, and has called him names ever since.' She extended her hand. 'Iris Abberton. You must be Petunia's nieces. She speaks of you constantly. And are you Petunia's brother Jonathon?' she asked the baron.

The baron glowered. 'I am Baron Thistledown.' Charlise felt her smile freeze and fix itself in place as Elise smothered a giggle. In their few meetings, she'd already learnt that he liked to be recognised, and hated to introduce himself. His moustache twitched as his brows pulled together, but thankfully, when he spoke, his tone remained polite. 'Charlise is my fiancée.'

'Of course, the Christmas Eve wedding!' Iris said, her eyes lighting in recollection. 'It's very... unique of you both.'

Was her upcoming wedding the subject of conversation even here, on the opposite side of London? If only she could slink into the shadows and hide. Charlise's father had hoped that the excitement of Christmas might divert people's attentions from her nuptials, but now it seemed that the opposite was true.

'I hope you will be able to attend our gathering then, all of you,' Iris continued, speaking in a rush, either not noticing or deliberately ignoring the baron's scowl. 'I would have written, but I do not have time for stationary. We are about to go abroad again, and Papa wants to celebrate the festive season. He has convinced his grace to host a Christmas party in his ballroom on the twenty-third. How he manages such a thing when the duke can barely stand his club, I'll never know.' She shook her head, smiling affectionately. 'I need entertainment. And don't even mention the catering. Say you'll bring your troop to sing, Petunia, it will be such fun. Papa has invited all his friends. Miss Delaney has promised to perform, and the Hempels are practically a party on their own.' As she spoke, she gave an unconscious gesture towards other residences in the street. 'Speaking of which, here comes Mr Hempel. Lawrence!' she called, bunching her skirts before darting off down the path.

'Abberton... of Abberton Trading.' The baron rolled the words in his mouth, as if sampling them to see how they suited his taste. His gaze flicked to the house across the street, then further down the road, to the grand sandstone villa at Number 10. 'And his grace... Miss Hartright, you have quite a prestigious address. Many of your neighbours are men of significant social stature.'

Aunt Petunia gave the baron a polite nod and a thin smile. 'Thank you, your lordship, but I did not choose my new home for the men it would bring me into the orbit of. This address is for my convenience.'

'Of course, of course,' he said. 'But you cannot deny, your neighbours are *fascinating*. Charlise! On Christmas Eve, dress here. It's so close to the chapel.'

'Here?' Charlise looked up at the towering white façade. Her aunt's townhouse was lovely, but the windows opened into strange rooms that she had never set foot in. 'I had planned to dress at home. I thought it may help me feel closer to my mother.'

He waved his hand in dismissal. 'Memories are portable, are they not? Besides, a wedding is about new beginnings, not focusing on the past. That's what you want, isn't it? To forget the past?' His tone twisted from debonair to dark, heavy with unsaid things.

Charlise scrunched her skirt in her hands and lowered her gaze to his shoes, before chancing a glance at her aunt. 'If Aunt Petunia agrees?'

'My darling girls are always welcome at my home. Why don't you stay all week? It will make rehearsals easier, and you can attend Abberton's gathering. I'll send a message to Jonathan. Thank you for your escort this afternoon, your lordship. It is time we prepared for our concert.'

'May I first have a private word with my fiancée?' he asked.

Aunt Petunia had never shared what she thought about the baron, at least not with Charlise directly. All afternoon as they circled the park, she'd kept a neutral face in conversation with him, but now, with a potential delay to the evening performance looming, annoyance flickered in her eyes.

'Charlise, don't stay out too long.' Aunt Petunia placed a guiding hand on Elise's back, and the two of them ascended the steps before crossing into the buttercup yellow entry, nattering about what shade of blue might suit the door.

With the sun retreating, the chill air began to drape, and its embrace settled on her shoulders. Charlise pulled her shawl tighter. She'd had so few private conversations with the man she was to marry.

'Have you been rehearsing?' The baron had withdrawn his watch from the pocket of his yellow coat and didn't look up as he studied its face.

'Everyday,' Charlise said, clutching her skirts again. 'Before breakfast and after lunch—'

'Because people will be watching.' He snapped the watch closed then turned his focus on her. 'I want you perfect, my songbird.'

She blended her hands into one another. 'I am not accustomed to singing alone.'

'Perfect, Charlise. You reflect on me now. Make sure the visage is pleasing.' And in two quick steps, he crossed the pavement and ascended into the cab, snapped the door shut, and rattled away.

From the bottom of the stairs, Charlise watched until the little conveyance rounded the corner, releasing an unconsciously held breath as it slipped out of sight. Through Aunt Petunia's address, she'd risen a little higher in his estimation of her. Surely, in the days to come, that would count for something.

'Charlise!' her sister called from the door. 'Come in before you catch a cold.'

Charlise ascended the stairs and stepped over the threshold into the entrance. Tiled in a black and white mosaic and lit by a glass gas lamp mounted above the sideboard, the room was almost the same size as the bedroom her and Elise shared.

'Welcome, my lovelies, welcome,' Aunt Petunia announced. 'We do not have time for a proper tour, so listen closely. Kitchens are in the basement. This level is the entry, and the dining room. Upstairs is the drawing room and library, and above that, my private rooms.' Their aunt gave them a meaningful glare that seemed to scream, *Don't even think of entering my domain*, before she swirled, her green skirts hushing. 'On the fourth floor are rooms for guests. You girls can share, as no doubt your father will join us. The upper rooms on the fifth floor are for housekeeping.'

Elise slapped her arm. 'First one there chooses beds!' Then she tore past, her boots thumping against the carpet runner that lined the stairs.

'I am not a child, Elise. I am twenty-one. I do not race for my bed.' Charlise took the first few steps at a slower, more dignified pace.

One floor above, Elise leant into the stairwell, her blonde hair spilling over one shoulder. 'You won't mind if I take the bed closest to the window, then?'

'You know I cannot sleep well by the door,' Charlise grumbled, one foot stomping.

'Well...' Elise's voice floated into the cavity, light and taunting. 'You had better get there before me.'

Elise's fast footsteps echoed. Charlise chewed her lip. She was supposed to be a grown up. She was about to be married, for heaven's sake.

'I bet the bed by the window has a wonderful view of the street.'

'Don't you even dare—' and without another thought, Charlise grasped the banister and lunged up the stairs.

Her rubber heels pounded as she jogged after her sister, and with the exertion, a hint of old memories returned. The muffled thud of each step could have been the thwack of a conker against her coat, or the tumble of chestnuts tipped from her skirt into a bowl, all the melodies of their childhood. She rounded the landing and moved faster, and above, Elise squealed, sounding just like how she had laughed when she was still toddling, and their mother had chased them from room to room during games of blind man's bluff. Charlise had always been good at energetic games, at running and play, only having her activities curtailed after Mother had passed and Father became concerned about her womanly constitution.

'Constitution be damned,' Charlise muttered to herself, then took a deep breath, bunched her muscles, and forced herself onwards. She grasped the banister and swung up the next flight, overtaking Elise as she went. At the next landing, she almost vaulted up the stairs to the fifth floor, but then she caught sight of a bright blue and lace bedspread and walls painted rose pink, and she changed direction. Once in the room, she launched herself and landed nose first onto the cotton quilt of the bed by the window, light with an abandon she hadn't known in years. Elise, her flagging steps clomping, flopped onto the bed by the door.

'I knew you could still outrun me.' As the laughter faded from her breath, Elise rolled onto her side. 'I'll miss you so much once you're married.'

Elise's chest was settling into a steadier rhythm as she caught her breath. Her long hair spilled around her, the loose hair of a young woman not yet debuted, although her emerald eyes held such wit and wisdom they could have been Mother's.

'We shall still see each other,' Charlise said lightly, brushing off the weight of the conversation. 'I'll be mistress of my own house. I am sure the baron will allow you to visit whenever you like. You'll be his sister, too.'

Elise stuck out her tongue. 'I am quite content with just you as my sibling. And with the dowry you're bringing, he should let you do whatever you wish. It's a wonder the duke at the end of the street didn't propose.'

'I have no ambition to be a duchess,' Charlise countered.

Elise rolled onto her stomach. 'Only a princess.'

Charlise opened her mouth in disagreement, but then giggled, enjoying the return of the shared intimacy that had been lost over the past few months. As young girls, they had often played at being princesses held captive in towers guarded by dragons, waiting for a dashing knight to rescue them.

'Although, if he had set his mind to it, I'm sure Father could have secured you a prince. It's a wonder he settled for a baron.' While she spoke with lightness, bitterness underlaid Elise's words.

The familiar knot in Charlise's stomach retied itself. 'He has ambition. He imagines a higher station for us.'

'He imagines for you,' Elise countered, swinging herself upright and planting her boots on the floor. 'You are a beauty, Charlise. I am not. Stop imagining that his love settles as level as water.'

Charlise wanted to draw her sister close. To tell her she was the most delightful, beautiful person in the city. But with her razor-sharp wit, there was no point arguing with Elise. She would only dismiss her compliments, as she always did.

'Do you love him?' Elise asked, her voice veiled in caution, like so many of their conversations since the banns were read.

'Not yet. But maybe, with time, love will grow.' Charlise pushed herself from the bed, turning to smooth the quilt. 'He loves music. Is very well read. And didn't Mother always say love takes a turn when a man and woman share a house? Hope to heavens, our turn is towards happiness.'

Would it be enough? The music, the books, the small compliments. When he possessed her and her dowry, when he claimed her as a husband did, would he be content? But what choice did she have? He had accepted her, and her shortcomings, and in doing so would raise her up to be a baroness.

'Didn't you imagine it all being different? Didn't you think being courted might be special? Even a little bit magical?' Elise asked.

'It's not uncommon for a man to approach a girl's father before asking her hand,' Charlise replied, ignoring the sting of the memory of her father delivering the news of her betrothal to her.

Somewhere below, the melodic rhythm of their names sounded. 'Charlise and Elise, time to go to the park.'

'It just...' Elise took a gulp of air before she squared her shoulders. 'It just feels like he bargained, rather than proposed.'

Charlise stiffened.

Elise adjusted her bonnet, neatening the ribbon beneath her chin, then left the room.

Charlise let the truth of her sister's words dissolve her rigidness before she sunk onto the bed. Bargained. Bartered. Reduced to a discount like a damp bolt of linen.

Ruined.

Her aunt's deep, demanding tone called again. Charlise checked herself in the mirror, then pushed a loose, dark curl under her bonnet.

'All will be well,' she assured her reflection. Her reflection looked doubtful. 'It will be. Just you wait.' Then, with a final tweak of her ribbon, she followed her sister down the stairs.

Chapter Two

Sinclair slung his canvas duffle over his shoulder and hoisted his old wooden crate onto his waist, its edges biting his hip. It clinked, half full with glass cordial bottles. He gave the little cabin one last sweeping look. Everything he owned sat on his back, and without his small assemblage of possessions—a few clothes, his shaving mirror and blade, his journal and portable pen, a stack of books, and the battered tobacco tin that held his greatest treasure—the room that had been his home for just over three months was once again a pale, wood-lined box of neutrality.

Without the rolling pitch of the sea, the ladder to the deck was easy to navigate. As Sinclair stepped into the crisp December air, his chest tightened as his lungs protested the sudden influx of cold. Even days after sailing into winter, his body struggled with the change, as if criticising him for the seasons being out of sync with the pattern he had known his whole life. December was supposed to be hot, the air blistering, and not like breathing inside an ice chest.

'Paymaster seen to you, lad?' Friedrich, the thickset ship's master of the merchant clipper, called as Sinclair stepped onto the deck. Broad and salt scarred, he walked with a thumping limp from his wooden leg, his slowness a façade—Sinclair knew that, in a storm, Friedrich could move a damn sight faster than any of the apprentices.

He tapped his coat pocket. 'All accounted for.' Against Friedrich's rough accent, Sinclair's words sounded stiff. His mother's insistence that he and his sister be educated had seen him spend many frustrated hours indoors at elocution, and try as he might, he could not shake the formality from his words.

Sinclair adjusted his bag, eyeing the narrow gangway that bridged the gap between the ship and land. Knocks, shouts, and clanging, the familiar activity of a busy dock amplified as it rolled over the water. Beyond, looming domes and steeples sat in silhouette against the faint glow of the city. And while he knew he should be eager to get ashore, a tight fear gripped him. On the long voyage—through each busy day of loading and unloading crates at different ports, seeing to swabbing and sails, and finally collapsing exhausted onto the lumpy horsehair stuffed mattress—there had been a comfort in knowing he floated over water that stretched all the way back home, even though each day the wind that filled the clipper's sails took him further away. This evening, for the first time in his life, he'd sleep over soil that wasn't Australia, and the distance suddenly felt very acute.

'You got somewhere to stay?' Friedrich leant against the rail. The wind ruffled his grey peppered hair as he looked across the port.

'I suppose I'll find a room at a boarding house or an inn. Try to get use of a kitchen so I can make and bottle some sherbets and syrups. Once I've some stock, I'll go selling door to door. That's how my old dad made his name.'

'Forgive me, lad. If it's one thing ship's masters don't do, it's pry,' Friedrich said, his voice thick with experience. 'Less known about the crew, the better. But I have to ask, if only to satisfy myself that you know the answer. Why'd you come halfway round the world to do what your father had already done? Why not just stay and work with him?'

Across the docks, a large crane swung out over a cargo ship, and small dots of men scurried clear. The crane hook lowered as they moved back, and while Sinclair could not see them in detail, he knew that they'd be tying knots, fixing hooks, and checking ropes. Men like himself, broad chested and hard as rock, although inside, he'd never felt more like a child. Why indeed? As he remembered the last words he'd exchanged with his father, the indignant flame flickered again. His frustration at being 24 and not given more responsibility, of being constantly overruled by his father and brothers, had finally resulted in an outburst which had been met by his father's stern Caledonian stubbornness, and instead of backing down like usual, Sinclair had thrown a few belongings into a pack and made for the first ship hiring deckhands at Hobsons Bay, even though he'd never been to sea before.

'Because I need to be my own man. Independent,' he said, reasserting the conviction that had filled him as he spluttered out his angry monologue before he walked out. 'Be more than McIntyre's son, or a McIntyre brother.'

'There are far worse fates than having a family and a name,' Friedrich said. 'You got plans? How are you going to spend Christmas?'

Sinclair shrugged. 'My grandma used to talk about going wassailing when she was a girl. I thought I might find a group to watch, get my bearings. Care to join me?'

Friedrich spluttered a laugh. 'A bunch of old women singing hymns? No thank you, although I might see if I can find a lady who'll do a bit of wailing for me.' He thrust out his hand, and Sinclair shook it. When he'd made the deal to cross the world as ship's steward, the hard grip had made him wince. Now, at the end of 102 days at sea, Sinclair met the man's strength. 'I'll be sad to see you go. It ain't often you find a man who can scale rigging and tally a ledger. You're a good worker, and that lemon syrup you make is one of the sweetest remedies to the wobblies as I've ever tasted.' He nodded at the assortment of glass bottles in the old crate. 'We'll be pushing out again in a few days, on Christmas Eve if the tide suits. If you change your mind, there'll be a bed on *Saint Anne* for you.' And with a nod, the ships master pulled his cap, then turned and limped back towards his cabin.

Sinclair readjusted his crate, the glass jangling, then set off over the gangway and into the semi-darkness of the wharf. He had traipsed Hobsons Bay and Sandridge, the biggest ports in Melbourne, since he was a boy, trailing after his father or older brothers, and the ship had stopped in docks during the voyage—first Sydney, then the tip of New Zealand, before heading onto Cape Horn, and then, traversing the Atlantic. But the Port of London seethed with a life and energy greater than all of them combined. Men rolled barrels, shouting and cussing, while cranes swivelled to extend over ships' decks, their wheels rolling over fixed tracks. Warehouses pointed triangle gables at the grey sky, and horses pulling drays and lorries lined the narrow, stinking alleyways.

He didn't know where he was heading, so he chose his path by ear, and with each step, he put the noise of the docks at his back and allowed himself to be led towards the sound of a city coming to life with evening.

Eventually, after dodging scampering children and keeping his head down to avoid the calls of street women, he came onto a bustling main street filled with coaches, wagons, sulkies, cabs, and pedestrians. Sinclair's vision swam. Which direction? Where to go? A man knocked against him as his arm stretched, and a large coach pulled by four haggard draught horses eased, then stopped. People were squashed so tight inside that they seemed about to burst from the windows. Some even sat perched on the roof. The man who had flung out his arm tossed a coin at the driver, then pulled himself inside the contrivance. Sinclair, clutching his crate, could only blink.

'Inside or knifeboard?' the driver shouted, his voice half lost to the clanging of horses' shoes and grinding wheels of passing coaches.

A ride through the city might help orient him. If nothing else, it would give him a chance to settle the squall in his stomach.

'What's the cheapest?' Sinclair called.

The driver grumped a laugh. 'Depends on where you're headed.'

'I don't know,' he replied. Emptiness, as cold as the wind gusting down the thoroughfare, twinged in his chest. He shifted to better balance his load, and the little tobacco tin pushed into his chest. 'On second thought,' he shouted at the driver. 'I'd like to see some wassailing.'

CHAPTER THREE

A snowflake.

As Charlise counted the beats for the chorus, she watched it float languidly through the air. The small white speck suspended in the lamplight hovered over the audience as if searching. It might be a sign that this year would be a white Christmas, just like in the books she had read as a child when snuggled into her mother's side. She might wake to a London that resembled the magical scenes depicted on the Christmas cards she sent, instead of the soot-weighted dankness she experienced each day.

Charlise brushed the fanciful notion away. It never snowed at Christmas. Not here. Not anymore.

Still, the little white fleck persisted to dance, unnoticed by the gathering. A decent group were watching this evening, too. Aunt Petunia would be happy, even though most of the audience were friends and family. Such details didn't bother their aunt as long as her choir sang on point and the applause was audible.

Charlise turned the page in her hymn book. Towards the back of the group, a man, slightly taller than most, paused. His form a silhouette, he stooped to deposit something on the ground, then stepped into a small ring of yellow light beneath the gas lamp, and Charlise's breath caught so sharp she had to mouth the next few words in the song. She pressed her hand to her stomach and forced herself to inhale.

He held himself so casually, like he knew his place in the world was at the back of the crowd, and rather than forcing himself into thin voids where he was not wanted, accepted it with grace. Broad, wearing a black suit that even in the low light she could tell was worn, his ash blonde hair sneaking from beneath a flat cap, he leant against the lamppost and crossed his arms, tipped his head, and smiled.

The snowflake gave one last flitter, then settled on his shoulder.

'Are you ready?' Elise jutted her elbow into Charlise's side.

'I think so,' Charlise whispered, drawing her eyes from the man and refocusing on Aunt Petunia. She took a long inhalation, rolled her shoulders, and relaxed her torso, as she had practised a hundred times, a thousand times before. *Drawing rooms are not available for you*, her father had snapped as he slapped his hand against the piano lid. *You will need to be better than most ladies if you are to hold the baron's attention.* Charlise tried to follow her aunt's steady conducting, but like the snowflake, her attention drifted back to the beautiful tall man, just to check if he was still there. And he was. Watching them. Watching her.

The crowd shifted, and a few coughs and grunts filled the air. The baron edged forward, his gaze narrowing.

Charlise took a breath that failed to banish her jitters, clasped her sister's hand, and began to sing.

As we watched at dead of night,
Lo, we saw a wondrous light.

She should have sung her lines to the baron, she knew, but her gaze dragged to the man at the back, the ring of light kissing him like a halo, and as she sang, his affable grin lit into an expression she could only describe as wondrous. A magic crept through her, that glowing fizz that suffused the air only at Christmas, and with an indistinct flash, images of Mother's arm around her shoulder, Elise snuggled into her side, and the worn pages of *The Nutcracker* glittered in her memory.

But just as those days had cracked, so did the sparkle of the moment fade as the man looked over his shoulder and into the park. A part of her cried out as the beauty of the connection slipped. She tried to call it back with another line, but the chorus joined in, and he stepped from the lamplight and into the evening fog.

It was only after she lost sight of him that Charlise registered the screaming.

CHAPTER FOUR

Sinclair hadn't heard the song before. It must be new and yet to make its way across the seas. Everyone at home sang carols at Christmas, usually loudly, as if trying to bridge the gap between the antipodes and the opposite side of the world. Every Christmas Day, dressed in their best clothes, they all huddled around the piano and belted out tunes like, *O Christmas Tree* or *The Holly and the Ivy*, pretending they weren't drenched in sweat as the thermometer edged past a hundred degrees.

The coach driver had deposited him here and pointed across the park. 'Carollers,' he had shouted.

'And accommodations?' Sinclair asked, but the driver was already on his box, whip flicking, his whistle urging the horses into action. At a loss for what else to do, he had wandered across the park to the choir, found a spot at the edge of the crowd, and settled his crate at his feet.

A beat, a note, a soloist took up the tune, and he was lost.

Her delicate pink lips slipped over each note in a breathy embrace, a soft blush brushed her cheeks, and dammit if he couldn't shake the feeling that she was singing to *him*, as if she understood the loneliness in his heart at being so far from home. The words were meant to be joyful, yet a melancholy attached itself to her melody. She reminded him of a trapped bird who knew it had been caught, and instead of fretting against the bars in search of an escape, only sought to enjoy its last few moments of peace before its wings were clipped.

A shout came from behind. Sinclair turned, reluctantly, but an instinct for trouble honed by years in the warehouse had taught him that ignorance rarely led to bliss. Another shout, followed by a call of, 'Settle, you daft horse!' He searched the path, hampered by the eerie hue of mist.

Ahead, a young bay clattered through the park, dragging an empty two-wheeled sulky in its wake, and, judging by its high whinny, it was frightened. He'd seen horses like this before. Good horses, but too young, taken straight from farms and put to work in a busy city before they'd had time to grow accustomed to noise and bustle. They shied at every bang or shout until their fear drove them to bolt, and to make things worse, whatever dolt owned her hadn't even thought to use blinkers. The poor animal tossed its head, then lunged forward, and the wheels of the sulky cleared the kerb before careening into the park at a terrifying speed, and to his horror, headed straight towards the carollers.

Sinclair, eyes on the horse, ran into the dark, and as it came alongside him, he took up its pace. Normally, he'd try to corral it into a corner, but the park was too wide, the paths too busy. Legs pumping, his duffle rubbing against his back, he reached, breath huffing, and stretched with all his might to scratch at the bridle and grasp the leather, clenching tight.

The horse, mist huffing from its nostrils, made to rear, but the sulky stalled its movement. Hooves clattered as its shoes clipped the path, and Sinclair gripped the bridle tighter, this time cooing, 'Settle, girl. No one's going to hurt you.' She tossed her head, but he resisted the show of independence. 'Enough of that,' he said, rubbing her neck. 'That a girl.'

Calming horses, or disgruntled workers, or, if an order had
been delayed, his father, had been a daily occurrence in Sinclair's
life before he left home. Overseeing the ground floor at the
biggest cordial merchant in Melbourne did not allow the luxury of
self-aggrandisement. Normally, after the problem had been solved, he
simply returned to his day, so it took a long moment for him to register
the smattering of applause and the calls of, 'Good show.' From the
small crowd, a woman, the choir conductor, raced forward, her bright
green skirts catching the lamplight. The horse shook its head with
unease, and Sinclair instinctively placed a protective hand on its nose.
The conductor stalled, then continued at a slower step.

'Heavens,' she said with a quiet awe. 'I believe you have saved my
life, and the lives of my dear choir.'

'Do you know who owns her?' Sinclair spoke quietly, but a ferocity
filled his tone as he looked around the crowd. At home, good horses
were too scarce, and he hated seeing even the draught horses given
grief. 'Whoever brought her into the city ought to be whipped!'

'Thank you for your assistance, young man.'

The crowd parted to make way for a tall, thin man dressed in blue
plaid pants and a long yellow coat.

Sinclair's hold on the rein tightened. 'She shouldn't be in the city,'
he said, struggling to keep his voice low.

'How else will she learn?' The man laughed, then tilted his head
quizzically. 'Do I hear a hint of the antipodes?'

'I've just arrived from Melbourne,' Sinclair said, not liking the
way the man said 'antipodes,' like even the word in his mouth was
unpleasant.

'Australia? My my, not a convict, are you? Where is my purse?'
Then he laughed, loud enough to cover the fact that only a few others
in the crowd joined in. 'My groom will take her now.'

The groom tugged at the mare's bridle, cursing under his breath. Reluctantly, Sinclair released his grip on the leather. He shuffled to the edge of the path as the horse and sulky turned in a wide arc.

Sinclair watched the man go, his chest tense with indignation. 'A horse like that needs care, not bullying,' he called, not giving a damn for the shocked expressions of the surrounding crowd, nor for the way the man stiffened and rounded back, his moustache twitching. 'Care. And respect.'

'I'll keep that in mind,' he drawled, then disappeared into the blackness beyond the gas lamps, his yellow coattails flicking.

A shiver ran through Sinclair as a cold gust slithered between the stretched weave of his coat, the action a reminder of the peculiar thrill he'd felt during the song. The soloist—where was she?

He scanned the cluster of full skirts and fine hats before spotting her a little way from the group, under the lamppost where he had left his crate. She stared into the dark, towards the daft man and his horse.

'Excuse me, miss,' he said, stepping closer. 'Are you hurt?'

She took a hurried step back. Her gloved hands grasped at one another, as if trying to save the other from drowning. 'You cannot speak with me,' she said in a rush. She looked over his shoulder, into the dark, then brushed her hands against her dress. 'I mean, it is not proper to address a lady you do not know.'

'Is there someone here who can introduce us?' he asked, looking around the crowd.

'You can only be introduced to a lady by someone you already know. And someone who is also an acquaintance to myself,' she said earnestly. 'It's proper etiquette, you know.'

He'd been lectured on such rules around behaviour at boarding school, but in his corner of the world, everyone mostly knew everyone, so he'd never had much use for them.

'Well, if that's how things are, I fear I must say farewell and return to the ship,' he replied.

'You're leaving?' Her haughtiness evaporated, replaced with shock. 'After coming all this way?'

'You have said I can only make a friend if there is someone who can introduce me. And as I know no one, I fear I am destined to not speak to another soul in this city. I may as well return to the sea, where the fishes do not require introductions.' He slapped at his side. 'Blast it.'

'What's the matter?' she asked, her beautiful dark eyes widening.

'The horse. She was my friend. I should have asked her to help me with introductions. But, alas, she is gone.'

Was that a smile? Ever so faint, her lips twitched into a grin, and the edges of her eyes creased. 'That is unfortunate. We are destined to remain strangers then.'

'I bid you good day, Miss What's Your Name.' He gave a flourishing bow, his arm sweeping wide.

'Until next time, Mr Galant Stranger,' she replied, biting her bottom lip, a mischievous twinkle in her eyes.

'Oh, my heavens.' The conductor bustled over and took up his hand, clearly not fussed by the same restrictions that had worried the soloist. The rest of the choir flocked around her, like ducklings scampering after their mother. 'Sir, we cannot thank you enough. I am Miss Petunia Hartright. Let me introduce my dear girls. This is my niece, Charlise Hartright, and her younger sister, Elise. Good heavens, that could be a poem, Charlise and Elise.' She chuckled to herself, then turned to the rest of the group. 'Lady Miranda Tatton, Miss Stephanie Wade, Miss Lilian Archer, Miss...'

As the exuberant Miss Hartright—conductor, Miss Hartright—continued to point out young ladies in the group, Sinclair felt his attention glaze, then drift. *Charlise*. His heart, so recently stilling from the excitement, gave a thump that sent a tingle through his chest to his stomach, and goodness, even lower. Having just come through 102 days at sea, and just a few of those in port, his mind lurched from trying to dredge up his boarding school lessons in gentlemanly behaviour to the bawdy tales passed from bunk to bunk after too many nights at sea, and with a sailor's crudeness, in his mind he had stripped Miss Charlise Hartright bare and lowered her into his bed.

'And, finally, Miss Rosanna Hempel, who is also my neighbour. And, how could I forget my baritone, Phineas Babbage?' The conductor took up Sinclair's hands again, squeezing firm. Her blue eyes sparkled, and with her warm smile, she reminded him of his grandmother. Kind, but also fierce. 'How can we repay you, Mr...'

'McIntyre. Sinclair McIntyre. Well...' he rubbed the back of his head, thinking. 'I have only just arrived. Can you recommend a boarding house? Or some decent accommodations?'

'Boarding house? No, no, no,' the elder Miss Hartright chastised, her finger waving. 'That will not do, not for our saviour. Mr Babbage!' she called. The baritone, who had been staring across the park, startled. 'Could you find yourself so charitable as to provide Mr McIntyre with a room?'

Chapter Five

'Quite the place you've got here.' Sinclair peeked into a small, sunlit room, the smell of toast and tea greeting him. Mr Babbage, only his neatly groomed dark hair visible behind his newspaper, sat at a small, round table laid with plates, butter, a teapot, and a small pile of toast. Pots of red jam and orange marmalade dotted the cloth, bright accompaniments to the otherwise stark setting. At the seat next to him sat a short-haired grey cat with dark green eyes, his white-tipped tail flicking. Without lowering his broadsheet, Mr Babbage reached for the milk jug, tipped a little into a saucer, then slid it across.

'What's your cat's name?' Sinclair lowered himself into a chair, leering at the cat as it lapped. He'd never shared a breakfast table with a feline before. He reached for the teapot, but before he could grasp the handle, a man in black livery stepped forward and swooped it from his grasp. Sinclair fidgeted uncomfortably until the man finished. He'd never had someone serve him tea before, either.

'Spencer. And he isn't my cat,' Babbage replied from behind his paper.

'Are you sure about that? Cats have a way, you know. My mum never wanted a cat in the house, couldn't bear the shedding, but then one turned up and refused to go, and next thing my sister had named her, and...'

The cat flicked an ear, its eyes narrowing. It looked bored. Could cats be bored? The cat Spencer spun in a tight circle, rested his front paws against the back of the chair, squared himself, then leapt up, his hind legs pushing the chair so forcefully it thumped against the table, before he landed on the ledge and disappeared through the window.

'If Spencer wanted to be owned, he would be. But he much prefers to grace each resident of the street with his presence as it suits him.' Mr Babbage folded his paper and placed it to one side. 'I trust you were comfortable?'

'Extremely. Much more comfortable than on the clipper. Thank you, Mr Babbage. You probably weren't expecting a house guest when you went to the park to sing.' Sinclair plucked at the tablecloth. 'And I suppose it would be rude of me to intrude a little more, but I was wondering, would you mind if I used your kitchen?'

Mr Babbage looked over his glasses, his dark eyes pinpoints sharply trained. Sinclair's host looked around the same age as Richard, the youngest of his three older brothers at around thirty. His mouse brown hair was neither neat nor untidy, his stature neither imposing nor weak. Sinclair supposed the man good looking, but not in such a way that would turn a lady's eye, not like Malcolm, his eldest brother. Everything about Mr Babbage seemed wholly average, and if he left the room, Sinclair couldn't be sure he'd be able to recall anything specific about the man. He was, on the whole, entirely forgettable.

'You may call me Phineas. Petunia Hartright is quite a force. I find it easier to float with her tide than resist it.' He checked his watch, then stood and buttoned his coat. He nodded at the man who had served tea. 'Felix will show you the kitchens. Keep everything clean. Stay out of locked rooms. Don't be an oaf.'

Sinclair stood as his host left the room, then sat back down, nervous excitement bubbling. A bed, a kitchen, and breakfast. It was more luck than he'd imagined possible. He placed a piece of toast on his plate, and with a quick look at Felix, who did not react, added a second.

'So what does Phineas do to have a place like this?' he asked before crunching into a bite of crisp toast with creamy butter.

'Mr Babbage is a bank clerk,' Felix replied.

'A clerk? Perhaps I should consider a career change. This house is amazing.'

Felix stifled a cough. 'You require use of the kitchens?'

'If it's no trouble.' Sinclair scooped up a sliver of red jam, accidentally leaving a glob of butter in the pot. Felix winced. Heavens, he'd need to get better at this if he was going to stay. 'But first, I should visit some family. Then I need to head to a market. Do you have a map?'

Some hours later, Sinclair stood at one end of Honeysuckle Street as he flipped between the pages of a *Bradshaw's Handbook for Tourists* he had found in Phineas's substantial library. 'Where are you, Honeysuckle Street?' he muttered, tracing the lines of Mayfair, the curve of the Thames, and the rough shape of Hyde Park, but found no label. If he didn't know where he was, how could he figure out where he was going?

'Mr McIntyre!' Sinclair turned towards the shout, and racing fast, her skirts dancing around her calves, came Elise, the youngest of the Miss Hartrights from the park. She skidded to a halt in front of him. 'Are you going sightseeing?' she asked with a nod at his book.

'Not quite. I'm trying to find the street,' he replied.

She laughed, high and bright but with a hint of depth, the laugh of a young girl on the edge of growing up. It reminded him of his sister, Sary, and with a pang, he realised that in all her life they'd never been apart at Christmas.

'You won't find Honeysuckle Street on a map. It doesn't fit. The street is too short, and the name too long. But the park at the end,' Elise said as she pointed towards the place where they had met the night before and tapped at a hatched and uneven oval on the page. 'Is just here. If you can find it, you can always find your way.'

'Elise don't run off. I need to keep track of—Oh. Mr McIntyre.'

The night before, as he lay in bed, Sinclair had sworn it must have been the low lamplight, or the mist, or that he hadn't known a woman's touch for some time, and he had likely conjured the form and elegance of Miss Charlise Hartright. How could a woman like that be real? But today, with the morning sun lighting her face, he saw that his memory hadn't been nearly flattering enough. She looked down, long eyelashes shielding soft dark eyes, her ebony hair pinned into submission and framing the soft blush of her full cheeks, and the sweetest, most kissable cherry red lips he had ever seen. She tucked away an imagined stray curl, her beige leather gloves warming fingers so fine that, if he held them, they would be swallowed in the palm of his hand.

Sinclair closed the book and thrust it under his arm. He ran his hand through his unkempt hair, cursing himself for not finding a barber, or at least asking Felix for a trim. 'Good morning, Miss Hartright. I trust I may speak with you this morning?'

'You may,' she said with a slight smirk, then held out her hand. 'We have been introduced, as unconventional as it was.'

Sinclair forced his mind into action and drew up the memory of when his brother Richard had started courting. 'You are a ray of warmth on this winter's day.' Bowing, he pressed his lips to her glove, inhaling as he did so, filling his lungs with roses and lemon.

She coughed, and when he looked up, her smile had transformed into a frown. 'The proper etiquette is to shake my hand, Mr McIntyre.'

'Oh, blast it.' Sinclair straightened, slipped his palm against hers, and gave her hand a firm shake. 'Like so?'

'Goodness, I am not a dock worker,' she said, pulling back, but as she did so, she laughed, her tone flecked with mock indignity. 'Let us hope you are intended for company that does not mind such things.'

'I can't imagine the folk where I am headed will mind my manners, or lack of. I'm trying to work out how to get to Kensal Green.'

Like a branch crack, she stopped laughing and placed her hand to her chest. All the lightness that had surrounded them dissipated like a spoon of sugar in tea. 'Kensal Green?' she whispered.

'Did I say something wrong again?' he asked, looking between the two of them. 'Bloody hell, I'll never get this right. Oh blast, I mean—'

Elise sidled against her sister, entwining their arms. 'Our mother's buried there,' Charlise explained, her voice thin. 'It's our first Christmas out of mourning. Even though she's been gone two years, without her, this Christmas feels different.'

'It's my first Christmas without my grandmother. I know it's not the same as a mother. But she ah...she was quite special.' Grief, old and aching, hung between them, and the silence blossomed with the comfort of understanding. He waved the travel book in the air. 'I'm sorry to have upset you. I'll find my way, I'm sure. Good day, ladies.'

At least remembering to tip his hat, Sinclair gave the Miss Hartrights a nod and set off towards the park. When Babbage had told him not to be an oaf, he'd assumed he meant lying about with his boots on the furniture or coming back to Number 1 soused. He didn't think a conversation with two young women in broad daylight would be such a hazardous thing to negotiate.

The clap of boots on stone followed, and before he could turn, young Elise barged playfully against his side, sending him three steps off course. 'We'll show you the way,' she said.

'Are you certain?' He directed his question at Elise, but really, it was meant for Charlise. 'We won't break some rule I'm not aware of?'

Charlise took a step closer, a mischievous grin on her lips. 'At least three. Maybe five,' she said before her smile faded. 'No one should make a Christmas visit to Kensal Green alone. Now put your book away, we shall catch an omnibus. I am not walking all that way in these boots.'

The small field of green grass and stone slabs, which had once been at the edge of the bustling expanse of London, lay tucked behind a tall white arch. Progress nibbled at its edges, but inside Kensal Green cemetery, the congestion and noise of the city seemed to have been banished. The black fingers of branches stretched across the grey sky, and beneath their feet, the matted brown of decomposing autumn leaves muffled each step. Angels. Oak leaves. Sphinxes. Grecian urns. Simple columns. The sculptures of the dead jarred, not because they were alien, but because they were so similar to the graves that surrounded his grandmother where she was buried at Melbourne General Cemetery.

'What name?' Elise called, her voice echoing into the crisp silence. 'Brown,' Sinclair replied.

Elise turned, hands on hips. 'What other name. A Christian name.'

'Mary.' Sinclair tapped at the tobacco tin secreted in his coat pocket. 'Same as my grandma's name, and my mother.'

Elise ran off again. Beside him, Charlise slowed to his pace. Occasionally, the rhythm of their walk caused them to nudge one another, and each brush of her body against his sent a shimmer through him.

If the world were a page, she was a poem imprinted. No, not a poem, a song. She moved like notes lived in her, and as he fell into step, he could feel the beat, *step, step, step, step,* while his heart thudded louder and in its own silent tune, *ba-boom, ba-bing*. Dappled shadows danced over her gown, and thin fingers of mottled grey and light snaked through her hair.

'My sister was meant to be named Mary, to keep the tradition going,' he said, knowing he was veering into babbling but unable to stop. 'But my brother Richard kept calling her Scary Mary because she cried so much. When my dad went to register her birth, he stopped to celebrate on the way, and when he came home, it turned out he'd registered her as Sary by mistake.'

He buried his hands in his coat pockets, regretted his lack of gloves, and studied the dates on the headstones that they passed, then stole a glance, his cheeks warming as they both slung a look at one another in the same instance, only to look away, embarrassed.

'I liked your wailing,' he blurted out, then winced. 'I mean, your wassailing. Last night. Before that daft man's horse got loose, I was mesmerised.'

Her lips broke into a shy smile. 'No one says wassailing anymore. We're just carollers. It's my aunt's ensemble. She's very passionate about music and singing. She was in a choir with my mother. It's how her and my father met.'

'Love at first lyric?' he asked, his skin tingling at the thought.

'Not quite,' she quipped back. 'But, in time, yes. He adored her.'

I could adore you, Sinclair thought, his gaze trailing the naked grace of her nape, inching to the tickle of fur on her coat collar. *At least twice a night.*

He coughed, then rubbed his knuckles over his forehead. The more he tried to act like a well-mannered gent, the bigger an oaf he seemed intent on becoming.

'Over here,' Elise called from a few rows over, and Sinclair followed her voice. 'Mary Brown, 1835. Phillip Brown, 1837. Parents of Mary. Gone but not forgotten. Is it them?'

'Does it really say that?' he asked.

'Come see,' Elise replied.

Gone but not forgotten. His mother had chosen the same line for his grandmother, complete with an English rose carved into the top of the headstone, almost identical to the design that stared back at him in this freezing English yard so very far from home.

'My grandmother was a convict.' The words scratched out of him, as harsh as their history. 'She couldn't write, so she had the priest help her send letters home, but the only reply she ever got back was from the vicar telling her they'd died and been buried here. She thought they'd forsaken her. But maybe, reading that stone, they didn't.' He reached into his pocket and pulled out the tobacco tin, then pushed his nails against the tin lip, and, fingers tensing, cracked the little container open.

CHAPTER SIX

What beautiful hands he had. Not soft or lithe from doing nothing more vexatious than holding a pen, or a hand of cards, but firm hands, built from work. Thin veins snaked over their back, a hard worn nail flush against a slightly rough thumb, and while every inch of them spoke of effort and might, he held the tin like a child might raise up a favourite toy, or a comforting blanket. Charlise couldn't help but lean closer, desperate to learn a little more of this man that was three parts hard as macadam and one part soft as flannel.

'My grandma's last words to me,' he said, his voice an ache. 'Before she slipped away, she made me promise I would one day bring a piece of her home.' Nestled in the tin lay a delicate silver hook of grey hair tied with a thin blue ribbon. His finger grazed, barely touching it, his face distorting into a mix of pain spliced with love. 'It was the last thing she ever said.'

He squatted at the base of the grave and scratched at the ground, carving out a little cavity in the dark soil, his movements mechanical. Dirt caught along the sides of his fingers and beneath his nails. Charlise stripped her gloves, knelt beside him, and clawed at the earth with him. Cold, almost frozen and rough with grit, the soil rubbed hard, refreshing in its rawness. How many holes had they dug to plant roses as children, how many weeds had they pulled in the garden? How much distance had been placed between her and the beauty of the ground since her mother's loss? Charlise scooped out one last handful of tumbling soil, then heaped it into a little pile. Sinclair placed the lock in the depression, then kissed his fingers and raised them to the sky. 'In the next life, Mary Brown,' he whispered, and with a firm shove, heaped the dirt over.

He remained still, sitting back on his heels, head bowed. The wind whispered through the few remaining leaves and ruffled his hair. Charlise let the coldness infiltrate her, and the frostiness made her fingers tingle. If she stayed here, would she turn to ice? Perhaps she would become a statue amongst the angels, bowing her head in repentance, praying for the redemption that would only come at the end of a church aisle.

A cheerful trill broke the silence. Above them, a robin chirped as it hopped between branches and little plumes of mist escaped from its beak. Another bird called back in reply, and the pair of red breasts bounced between the naked branches before taking wing to the other side of the path.

'I think she's happy,' Elise said, following the flight of the birds across the cemetery, a smile in her voice, even though it carried a weight beyond her years. 'Do you think that's your grandfather flying with her?'

Sinclair huffed a laugh as he stood and brushed the dirt from his palms. 'I doubt it. She ah...she didn't know him that well. Actually, I'm not sure she knew him at all.'

'How could she not—'

'We really should leave Mr McIntyre to his morning.' Charlise interrupted her sister, trying to send her a message to hold her tongue. Realisation lit Elise's expression.

Sinclair shoved his hands into his pocket. 'It doesn't bother me. My grandmother's story, and my mother not having a father. Well, not one that gave her a name.'

Charlise's cheeks burned hot as she tried to find the right etiquette to cover a blunder like the one she had just made. How many books had she pored over, how many lessons from father to ensure she wouldn't stand out in a parlour once she entered society? Nothing she had learned covered what to do when someone wasn't embarrassed about such things, yet she had just told him he should be.

An unconventional situation called for an unconventional answer. She stood, then held out her elbow. 'Why don't you escort us to the gates, and tell us about her on the way?'

Strips of light crossed Charlise's skirts as they strolled, while Elise flitted along the path as light as one of the robins. For a man not wearing gloves, heat still beat from his light hold around her bicep, each tiny indentation of his fingers like a brand through her sleeve. A warm fizzle traced her spine. She should declare herself promised, but apart from accepting their offer of assistance, what right did she have to assume he thought anything more of her? Would she embarrass him again with her arrogance?

And she couldn't shake the thought that perhaps, if everything hadn't gone so horribly wrong, this is what courting would have been like. All shy smiles and fumbled etiquette.

Was there any harm in just enjoying this moment?

'I'd prefer you call me Sinclair,' he said, his voice a warm drizzle through the cold air. 'My father is Mr McIntyre. It doesn't sound right to my ears.'

'Call me Charlise,' she said, half turning towards him. 'Your grandmother sounds fascinating.'

He laughed, and she could hear the easing of the burden in his voice. 'She was something. I suppose she had to be. She was transported at eighteen.'

'Because of her...relationships?'

'That came later,' he said, shaking his head. 'And I think it was just one or two red coat gents she became friendly with. Just enough to help her get by. Her crime was breaking stocking machines, in Leicestershire, when steam engines put families out of work. She was protesting the changes that made her family homeless and drove whole villages into the city to look for work. But if you think my grandmother is something, she's barely a speck on my mother,' he continued, his voice thick with pride. 'She was sixteen when she married my father, and only a few years older than the boys she was to become a mother to. And they gave her a time. But she stuck with it. And now, they're like a bunch of kittens around her. Meek as you please.'

'Was your father transported too?' she asked, her curiosity edging out all thoughts of proper conversation.

'No, although he may as well have been for all the choice he and his first wife had. The laird had the whole village cleared out and paid everyone's passage to the other side of the world. A new start, he said, even though they'd never wanted to go.'

'So the illustrious heritage of Sinclair McIntyre includes a rebellious convict grandmother from Leicestershire, an illegitimate mother, and a Scottish father turned out in the Clearances.' She tapped off each point as she spoke. He was a mismatch of composite parts, every single piece at odds with what was considered respectable and desirous to men like her father, and the baron. Yet, she'd never felt more comfortable in another's company. 'And you sound like any gent I've met in a ballroom.'

'My mother insisted Sary and I be educated. Not at home, like the boys.' His rounded accent, formal English tinted with the odd clipped words, settled into the confession. 'We're quite the conversation at home. My mother, sounding as rough as any street urchin, and my father and brothers' brogues as thick as if they'd just walked out the highlands, and Sary and I, like a proper pair of toffs, even though she spends her days bottling and boiling in the kitchen, and I spend mine in the warehouse dodging horsesh—umm, dodging horses.'

They had reached the arch that marked the entrance to the cemetery. Inside Kensal Green, the outside world seemed prohibited. As they approached, the noise of the city clarified, and Charlise hung back, feigning waiting for Elise, but really, not wanting to rejoin the world beyond. Here, in the steady comfort of the parklands, she could forget everything and just be a young woman walking in the company of a new friend, who was young, and handsome, and had opportunity before him. Even with her sister as an unconventional, and perhaps slightly eyebrow raising, chaperone, she could imagine herself the young woman she might have been.

Elise skipped alongside them, spinning in a wide circle under the archway before turning back, her boots crunching in the gravel. 'What do you normally do for Christmas?' she asked.

'We sing, we eat. If the beach is calm, we swim,' he said.

'You don't ice skate?' Elise asked, her eyes widening.

'There isn't much ice when it's a hundred degrees.'

'What about building snowmen?'

'Truth be told, I've never seen snow.'

Charlise thought of the little snowflake that had circled the crowd and had somehow chosen him to settle on. A stiff wind blustered, and heavens be if a few stray flakes didn't catch on the breeze and circle around them. Sinclair followed their movements, his eyes dancing.

'Catch one,' Charlise said, chasing the few stray white flecks with her outstretched palm. 'Do you see it?'

Six long arms stretched from the centre of the flake, less than a quarter inch wide, its delicate web branching and connecting, before the ice melted into a droplet in her glove.

'They're so beautiful.' That same shy wonder from the night before sparkled in his expression. Sinclair held out his ungloved hand. Small flecks of dirt still clung to his thumb, and little flecks of snow landed alongside them. 'They reflect the light, like crystal,' he said, examining his catch. 'Look.'

As Charlise watched, the flakes melted, leaving little droplets of water that spread through the creases on his skin. She pulled her handkerchief from her pocket.

'They're all different,' she said as she wiped his palm. Through her gloves, she couldn't feel the heat of his body, but she felt his muscles first tense and then soften against her. Little plumes of mist flowered as she spoke, mingling with his. 'Not all are as pretty as those. Some are thin, like needles. Others are clumps. Some so small they are barely a speck. My mother always used to say that when you catch a perfect snowflake, you should make a wish.' Charlise chanced a glance up at him. 'What will you wish for?'

For a moment, the air between them remained frozen as she held her breath waiting for his answer. Of all the many things in the world, what would he want?

His thumb stroked hers, a brazen act she should not have allowed, but the pressure of his stroke felt so perfectly intimate, even through the barrier of her glove. 'I have a warm bed. A promise of toast each morning. And a new friend in a city full of strangers. You take it.'

'You're giving me your wish?' She couldn't help but smile.

He squeezed her hand gently, as if passing it to her. 'It's yours.'

It was just a silly game, and when they'd played it as children, she had wished for a new doll, or a pair of embroidered mittens with pink pom-poms on the wrists. But he watched her so expectedly, she couldn't help but feel that his gift carried magic, like the desires of her heart still mattered.

'Don't tell me.' He caressed her hand before lightly pinching her fingertips. 'Or it might not come true.'

'Not that anyone asked, but I would wish for a speedy ride home,' Elise said, her tone both mischievous and a warning. 'Or an omnibus. And what luck, because here comes one now.'

Charlise released Sinclair's hand and took a step back. How had she forgotten that they were in broad daylight? A bus led by sturdy draught horses pulled up, and a few passengers disgorged onto the kerb, chatting and laughing. Elise skipped up the stairs and took a seat by the window.

'Thank you for your help this morning, Charlise.' Sinclair removed his cap and gave her a nod. 'I hope your wish comes true.'

Charlise climbed the curved iron stair, a warmth in her chest, like the wish he had given her now lived there, beneath her ribs, next to the erratic thump of her heart. Beside her, Elise waved fast, and while she couldn't hear Sinclair's voice, she imagined the warm sound of his easy chuckle as he smiled, then waved back. Everyone always muttered that Elise needed to grow up, never quite seeing that she had grown up too much, too quickly.

What a simple joy to meet someone who saw Elise as she did.

Someone who understood the heavy pull of dark grief, but still delighted in catching a snowflake in his palm.

Someone with hands so rough he didn't bother with winter gloves, but with a touch as tender as a feather.

The little wish in her chest fluttered again, and its nervous tremor spread like a starburst. As the coach pulled away, Charlise craned to follow him through the windows. As he grew smaller, a slight yearning flowered as her wish took form.

And it wasn't very ladylike at all.

CHAPTER SEVEN

As Sinclair snapped a chunk off the dense sugar loaf, a few crystals scattered over the bench. He rubbed the sweet clump against the bright skin of the lemon he had bought the day before. Scratching and scraping against its skin, the sugar gradually absorbed its oils and turned yellow before crumbling onto the bench. He scooped up the little pile of raspings and scattered them in the pot, stirring until they dissolved into the syrup.

His second morning at Number 1 Honeysuckle Street had started much the same as his first. He had taken tea and toast with Phineas in the small breakfast alcove on the first floor. His host had made scant conversation but did not leave him feeling unwelcome. Phineas had gone to his employment, and Felix had shown him to the kitchens. He'd even helped him light a fire in the stove.

'Be good to see it used,' Felix said, his haughtiness making a slight shift to conversation. 'The most up-to-date facilities available and used for nothing more than tea and toast.'

'Does Mr Babbage not ever dine at home?' Sinclair asked.

'He prefers his club,' Felix replied, his tone again curt.

Having been raised in a city where every family held close the story of its origins, Sinclair knew better than to pry. Babbage's business was his own, and he was a guest. He had a soft bed, a fitted-out kitchen, and no intention of putting either of those at risk, no matter how curious he might be.

The syrup simmered, and he hoisted the pot and gave it a good swirl for luck, like his mother always did. A puff of citrus steam wafted up, sweet and just a little tart. He sat the pot back against the hotplate and pulled himself up to sit on the thick wooden bench top, swiping the book he'd borrowed from Babbage's library from its surface. *The Handbook of Etiquette: Being a Complete Guide to the Usages of Polite Society* may have only been a quarter of an inch thick, less than seventy pages, but it could have been a heavy tome for all the sense it made.

'Introductions. Dress. Dinner parties,' he flipped through the pages. 'So many rules.' He sat hunched over the book, trying to focus on the bland text as the syrup across from him spat and bubbled, but all the while his mind kept floating back to the lovely Charlise.

Just the name, the memory of her face, sent a warm jolt through him. He could have spent his entire day strolling through the shadows of the cemetery and listening to her lyrical voice, hanging off every melodic word, watching her lips, ruddy red in the cold, as she selected each phrase as if their conversation was a composition.

Before, at home, he'd had a few lady companions, and on the voyage, at their rare stops, he'd paid for some company with coin. And last night, alone in his bed, he'd thought of those intimacies, but instead imagined Charlise laying back against his sheets, opening her arms, pulling him into her embrace, and into her body.

The pot spat, and, with a jolt, he pushed himself from the bench and grabbed a towel, wrapping it around the pot handles before lifting it from the stove and setting it onto the board. He shook his head to break the lecherous hold of his thoughts. Purchasing the ingredients and bottles for this small amount of cordial had taken a heftier slug of his earnings than he had expected, and he could ill afford to let them burn while his mind meandered.

Sinclair grabbed a lemon, sliced it, then squeezed the juice into the pot. After a few moments of stirring, the liquid cleared. On the bench, six brand-new, cold-pressed green glass bottles sat waiting. Once the syrup had cooled, he slowly filled each one before stoppering them with a cork. He leant back to admire his morning's handiwork.

Not much, but a start.

Sinclair rolled his shirt sleeves down, then took up the etiquette book again.

Without persecuting, let them generally contrive to meet them once a day in their walks. The fair sex are very quick-sighted, and we do not doubt that the ladies will soon discover the impression made by their attractions...

'Contrive to meet them on their walks,' Sinclair muttered. 'I don't bloody well know when she walks.'

Sinclair eyed the bottles lined up along the bench before snatching one up and making for the stairs. 'But I can contrive something.'

Outside, a crisp winter sun forced itself between grey clouds. The air felt so frigid, it was a wonder the world hadn't turned to ice. Sinclair knocked on the door of Number 7. A tall man in a black suit answered.

'No hawkers,' he snapped and began to close the door.

'I am calling on Miss Hartright.' Sinclair spoke in a rush, bending to remain in view as the door swung shut. 'I have a gift.' He thrust the glass into the gap.

The man took the bottle by the neck. 'Cordial?'

'It's my trade. Best quality in all of Melbourne. I brought it to say thank you. Miss Hartright assisted me greatly.'

The man looked down, the corner of one lip lifting. 'Your trade.'

Indignity flashed in Sinclair's stomach, like at the park, when the man with the runaway horse had called him a convict. He wasn't embarrassed of his grandmother, and he certainly wasn't embarrassed by his work. He squared his shoulders and looked the man in the eye. 'I've come to London to start a business.'

There was something familiar about the man's features, the shape of his eyes, or perhaps the cut of his cheek bones, and with a crush, Sinclair realised that this man wasn't a butler, but Charlise and Elise's father. His mind raced back to the etiquette book, trying to draw forth something, any form of advice on how to behave. Should he wait for an introduction? No, that was only for ladies. Sinclair thrust out his palm. No man could resist an offered hand. 'Sinclair McIntyre.'

'Jonathan Hartright,' he said, briefly pressing Sinclair's hand. 'Is there a shortage of opportunities for drinking establishments in the colonies? My understanding was that there was plenty of demand.'

'I hope to grow it into something bigger. I'm going to be a self-made man.' Even as he spoke, old Friedrich's words rang in his ears, and doubt crept into his nerves. *Why'd you came halfway round the world to do what your father had already done?*

'Well. Best of luck. And all that.' The man turned, taking the bottle with him, and while Sinclair threw out a, 'Thank you, sir,' his meek attempt echoed unacknowledged into the hallway as the front door closed.

By three o'clock that afternoon, many more doors had been closed to him, and Sinclair felt that the only thing worse than London's sooty fog was the knots and swirls of its woodgrain.

He shuffled his crate, taking each step through the park a little slower. His bottles weighed ten times as much compared to when he'd set out, buoyed by optimism and ignorance. Homesickness shivered through him as the wind blew, again his body reminding him that the seasons were all wrong. He'd left as winter was easing, then sailed back into it. Ahead, the towering palatial villa, said to be home to some soprano he had never heard of, stood grey and water streaked. Across from it sat Babbage's place. Sinclair lowered himself onto one of the park benches, not quite ready to face the steely silence of Number 1.

There was a harsh edge to this city that he hadn't expected. And he didn't have endless days, or endless coin. While Babbage hadn't given him a date to leave by, the man's hospitality was unlikely to be endless. What if Friedrich left in a few days, and Sinclair had no income? No steady work? He'd be a homeless beggar, no better off than his grandmother before she'd been transported.

His mother had ensured he had an education, and his father had given him a trade. And he had thrown it back at them, and now he ached with his mistake.

He had no inheritance, no allowance, no credit. Who was he to have pride?

Rain drizzled. He pushed up his coat collar and tried to ignore it. In the park, a few black umbrellas popped into use. One man, his step visibly lifting into happiness as he looked ahead towards the street, threw a glance at Sinclair as he passed, then halted, before he took a few steps back and peered at him from beneath his umbrella.

'I know you. You're the man from the park who caught the horse. My daughter is in Miss Hartright's choir. You have my sincere thanks for your intervention.' He held out his hand. 'Lawrence Hempel.' Sinclair, lacking enthusiasm, gripped it but didn't stand. Probably another flagrant disrespect of this city's rules, but he was too tired to care.

'It really wasn't much—'

'You're staying with Babbage.' Hempel said the name of Sinclair's host with tightness. 'I won't hold that against you.' He nodded at the crate. 'Are you thirsty?'

Sinclair huffed a laugh. 'No, and it seems that no one else is either.' He pulled out a bottle and handed it to Lawrence. 'Take one. Best syrup in all Melbourne.'

Hempel unstoppered the flask and sniffed. 'It smells like a country garden. My wife will appreciate this. She's ahh... *in the family way*. Ale makes her ill. Poor woman, everything makes her ill.' Hempel's tone, previously so officious and brisk, softened as he spoke of his wife, heavy with unabashed affection. 'She's only like this when it's a girl.'

'My mother swore by ginger. In a cordial or a spritz. My dad said she drank it like a sailor in port swigs rum when she was carrying my sister and I. She makes it for all the ladies in the street when they're with child.'

'How much for a bottle?' Lawrence asked.

'Of this?' Sinclair pointed at the crate.

'Of the ginger.'

'I don't have any,' he said, regretfully. His fortunes finally looked about to turn, and he'd made the wrong bloody flavour. The brightness in Hempel's expression also dimmed. 'But I don't have much to do with myself this afternoon. It's simple ingredients, likely to be in any kitchen. It's how they're put together that matters. If you have a few spare flasks, I could come by and make a batch?'

'I couldn't impose,' he said, rain peppering his words.

'Ma would clip my ears if she knew I'd not helped an expecting mother,' Sinclair said. 'And after a day of failure, putting myself to good use would be welcome.'

Hempel weighed the proposition. 'Come along then. But I should warn you, life in Number 3 can be a little chaotic.'

Chapter Eight

When Horatio Carnall, thirteenth Baron of Thistledown, drank tea, his moustache whiskers partially submerged, and when they resurfaced, little beige drops clung to their tips.

The baron spoke, and while Charlise knew she should listen, she found it impossible to focus on anything but the tea. If he kissed her, would it be soggy and rough? Or like pressing her lips to a damp mop?

The baron rented small lodgings a few blocks from Mayfair, towards the river. Charlise had only been invited to visit once, three months earlier and with her father, when she had been introduced to the man put forward by the matchmaker. Since then, their occasional meetings had been in parks, or when she sang.

Beside her on the lounge, Elise reached for another biscuit, her third that morning. While she happily nibbled, as refined as she knew how to be, the baron's mother on the settee opposite raised her brows in disapproval, and even the maid rolled her eyes. Charlise wanted to remind them that Elise was a growing girl, as thin and lanky as a scarecrow, and a few biscuits were not likely to do her any harm. But she would need to negotiate a future with the baron's mother, and with the staff, as the maid that attended to her and Elise would stay with the Hartright family.

'Charlise, I have decided you should sing at this gathering. The one Abberton has invited us to,' the baron said, a few drops of tea still wobbling over his lips.

'I am singing,' she said, brightening. 'In the choir with my sister. Aunt Petunia has had us rehearsing each evening.'

'Not in the group. No one will see you, and I want everyone to see my beautiful bride. You will perform a solo. And besides, you want to make a good impression on your future neighbours.'

'But I get so nervous alone. And Miss Delaney, a real soprano, will be singing. I'm sure no one would want to listen to me.' The familiar fear that she would make some mistake filled her. 'Pardon, your lordship—my neighbours?'

He smiled with self-assuredness. 'I have bought Number 6.'

'The abandoned house?' For months, Charlise had been preparing herself for life at his small estate in the midlands. She'd only seen the place in a photograph. The idea of staying near her family and being across the road from Aunt Petunia was so unexpected, she almost cried out with joy.

'Obviously, it requires repairs,' he continued, examining his nails. 'So we will need to make arrangements for you until they are done. But I see our future unfolding on that street.'

The clock struck the hour. His mother pointedly looked at her watch.

'A good solid performance, yes?' he said as he rose, then led them to the door. 'Wear your new dress, the red one. I want everyone to see you shine.'

'Yes, your lordship.' She smiled, brighter than she meant to, and it was possibly too much, as he frowned quizzically. 'I look forward to it,' she said, tempering her enthusiasm, but inside her heart screamed. *Anything to make you proud, to make you happy, if it means I will have my sister close.* Charlise took Elise's hand and practically skipped with her sister's light youthfulness as they made their way towards the cab. As she placed her foot on the stairs, she tightened her coat, before realising she'd left her scarf in the hall. 'Wait here,' she said to Elise, who was already snuggling into her corner. 'I will only be a moment.'

Charlise tapped lightly at the baron's door, but when no one came, she pushed it open ever so gently. Her scarf sat on the entry table where she'd placed it as she checked her bonnet. She crept over the threshold.

'I drove by your little investment. It looks a fright. Are you certain her dowry will cover repairs?' The baroness's sharp voice was unmistakable.

'It was quite the bargain, considering it's such an esteemed address,' the baron replied.

'That's what you said about your bride, but I am still not convinced.'

'She'll come good. That aunt of hers knows everyone, men of breeding, and men of means. Just imagine, the gatherings, the connection, the opportunities. It will almost make up for having to marry down.'

Silence followed by awkward clinking. The baroness gave an exasperated sigh.

'After you return from Brighton, she will join me at the estate. Someone needs to ensure she learns how to behave like a baroness before she's let loose on society. You will stay in town to oversee the renovations. Just don't go flaunting your bit of fluff under her aunt's nose. After your brother, I do not need the drama of another weepy bride.'

Charlise swallowed, the knot in her throat sliding and filling her stomach with ballast, but the heavy reality helped her keep balance, rather than making her topple.

It was not uncommon, especially among the nobility. And she supposed, somewhere inside, she had known he would be the sort of man to keep a mistress. She was far from naïve.

And her father had described the baron as a practical man. Not much of a romantic.

Even so, she had thought she might have a chance at building a marriage, if not based on love, then on respect. Perhaps, like her parents, they might even become something more, a strong union at the centre of a loving family.

But no.

Her dowry. Her beauty. Her voice.

Beyond that, she was irrelevant.

She waited to feel angry, or jealous, or anything. But no feeling emerged. Not only her heart, even her pride went numb.

Being numb was better.

Back in the carriage, Elise fidgeted with excitement. 'Between you and Aunt Petunia, I won't know who to visit. She'll be so excited when we tell her you can stay in her singing troupe.'

Charlise tucked her sister into her side, fortifying herself with her love, reminding herself of the future Elise would have in the light, away from her shadow. Elise rested her head on Charlise's shoulder, and she lowered herself so that the two of them slot together like puzzle pieces. She squeezed Elise against her. 'One last day. You and me.'

Elise sat up. 'What do you mean?'

'Tomorrow, we'll do anything you want. Punch and Judy in the park, the shop windows. All the things we haven't had time for. We'll have our own Christmas adventure.'

'Can we eat chestnuts?'

'Of course.'

'Go skating?'

'Anything you like.'

'I shall start a list.' Elise fumbled in her pocket and pulled out a small notebook and began scrawling. 'And why do you sound so final. You're getting married, not dying.'

While Elise spoke with the all-knowing tone of a girl of fourteen, Charlise couldn't help but feel her sister was very wrong indeed.

Chapter Nine

Grey streets, grey buildings, and a sky that wept more often than it shone, London was a monochrome city. No wonder the inhabitants flocked to the parks at even the slightest break in the weather.

Sinclair rearranged the small package under his arm as he walked. Having failed in his first contrivance to meet with Charlise again by delivering cordial, he had taken the little etiquette book's advice and gone on a haphazard ramble through the roads around Honeysuckle Street. He'd wound along the river, watching the ships in port, and even spotted *Saint Anne* as workers scaled the sides, making her ready to pull out in a few days. Then, he'd made his way to the high street, where he'd bought a Christmas card to post home to Sary, and at the grocer he'd bought another sugar loaf, ginger root, and lemon, along with cinnamon, cloves, and spices. As he'd walked, he had gotten an idea for a flavour, and he knew he'd not be able to shake the thought until he mixed and sampled it.

The air had warmed in the late afternoon, and as Sinclair crossed the little park, he heard a call. One of the young Hempel boys—Elliot—slid across the ice, waving. Sinclair quickly spotted the rest of the family, as they were all wearing bright red coats and scarves. He chuckled. The nanny who worked for the Hempels was a bright woman. They zoomed over the ice like robins on the wing, easy to spot despite their speed.

'Mr McIntyre!' Sinclair turned at the familiar call. Normally, the formal use of his surname grated, but there was something in the lightness of the young Miss Hartright's call that made her insistence on calling him Mister a mark of affection, rather than distant formality. She slid towards him, accompanied by Rosanna, the eldest Hempel child, ice flicking up in small specks beneath the blades as she pulled up before him, her hands outstretched to each side to keep balance. 'Have you been shopping?' she asked with a nod at his parcels.

'Just some ingredients and a card to post home.' He held up the thinly wrapped packet, scanning the skaters over Elise's shoulder. 'Your sister isn't here?'

Elise shook her head, but when she spoke, her tone was slightly probing. 'Does that make you sad?'

It did, but that information was best kept close. 'Of course not.' Elise raised a knowing eyebrow. Had he not sounded convincing? 'She'd only remind me of all the rules I was breaking, and I'd feel more out of place than I already do.'

'I beg your pardon?'

With a lurch, Sinclair spun fast, only to face the lovely Charlise. 'You said she wasn't here,' he muttered.

Elise giggled. 'She wasn't. She was over there, putting on her skates.'

'You cheeky—'

Laughing with her friend, Elise straightened and waved as she slid backwards on the ice and out of reach, before taking a half-turn and speeding off again.

'I don't make the rules, I simply follow them.' Against the crisp white of her fur-trimmed blue coat, Charlise's dark eyes glistened, and behind the terseness was a pinch of hurt.

'I was just saving pride. In truth, I am thrilled to see you.' His confession rolled off his tongue with more speed than was likely wise.

Her cheeks slightly coloured. 'You shouldn't say such things. It is not appropriate.'

'Since when is the truth an inappropriate thing?'

Now more than a flush, her cheeks turned as red as a ripe persimmon. 'You really shouldn't—'

'Why aren't you skating?' he asked, nodding at the steel and leather skates that hung in her hand, hoping to cut off her reprimand.

'I can't get the straps tight enough. I don't feel stable,' she said.

'I have never tied skates before, but after three months at sea, I can tie a knot. Maybe I could help?'

Hesitant, like a bird moving between a hedge and seeds on the ground, he could see her mind whirling as she calculated the appropriateness of it, all while watching the ice with longing.

'I'm fast with my fingers,' he said. 'You'll be gliding with those demon Hempels in no time.'

She gave him a thin grin. 'Thank you.' She moved to a nearby bench. 'There are little pins along the base. You need to push them onto the sole of my boot, and then tie the straps in a crisscross.'

Sinclair crouched before her. He took up one of the skates, angled it into position, and cupped her boot by the ankle before firmly pressing the pins into the rubber heel. Grasping the brown leather laces, he wrapped them over the arch of her foot, then reached behind her calves, his fingers accidentally skimming the edges of the lace ruffles on her drawers. He waited for her to scold, but when he glanced up, she was watching him, eyes wide.

'And I'm also a little scared,' she said.

'And with good sense. Knives are for kitchens, not boots.' He tied off the first lace, then a little more languidly than he should have, he cupped her just above the ankle, in the narrow space between leather and lace, before placing her foot on the ground. He rested the second boot on his thigh. 'Elise skates like she's flying. Are you not as confident?'

'I taught her. Can you believe it? But now, the idea of being out on the ice frightens me. What's it like to not be so scared all the time?'

'Truth be, I am scared.' He crossed the laces and wrapped them around her calves. 'I had a row with my family. I ran away, like a coward, instead of facing them, and I'm scared if I go home without having proved myself, they'll laugh at me. But I'm also terrified of failing and not seeing them again. And if I do go back, will life carry on the same as it was before I left, or will it be completely different? And I don't know which of those scares me more.'

The air between them grew heavy with understanding, a feeling he couldn't explain but saw in her eyes, in the slump of her shoulders, and in her downcast glance at her gloved hands. He wanted to draw her against him and tell her that, whatever weighed upon her, she would find the strength to face it. Instead, he stroked her calf, the smallest affection he could offer in so public a place. Her silk stocking ran smooth and warm under his thumb. A small puff of mist caught her slight gasp, but she didn't move, only held his gaze, a slight hunger glinting behind her sadness. Like at Kensal Green, the air between them fizzed.

Sinclair tugged on the lace. 'Is that too tight?' he asked.

'A little tighter,' she said, her voice half a whisper.

He gripped the ties and pulled hard before finishing the knot. 'It will hold firm but be easy to remove. Do you feel safe?'

Charlise planted her feet on the ground, delicately balancing on the sharp steel. She gripped the edge of the seat so tight, he thought she was going to change her mind. He gave her an encouraging smile, and with a small nod to herself, she pushed herself to standing. Sinclair held out his hand as support, and she wobbled for a moment, then found her centre of balance. As she stepped onto the ice, she released him, gliding a few tentative feet away, then with a determined lunge, she leant forward and pushed off, now moving a little faster, and a little surer.

'For what it's worth,' she called as she spun, sliding backwards like Elise had. 'I think you are quite brave to try and stand on your own.' She turned, and before he could blink, she was nothing more than a blur of blue and white moving across the ice.

With each stride, the slight stiffness that she had carried rolled off her shoulders. Tensions rippled out of her, as visible as the wind that tickled her skirts. Sinclair followed her path, then gradually clocked the tilt of heads that turned in her direction, men whose eyes trailed away from their conversation as she passed. His grandmother had once described a friend, a fellow convict, as *painfully beautiful*, and watching Charlise, he finally understood what she meant. So pleasing to the eye, her person ceased to matter. Meek, yet always drawing attention. And hadn't he been one of them? Hadn't he been enraptured by her face, her voice, at the park? But now, so much more drew him in. Her kindness. Her love for her sister. The slight wildness that seemed trapped by rules and propriety. If only he could carve out a space for her where she felt safe and give her room to fly.

But the memory of the man who'd answered the door, and his sneer when he'd mentioned his trade, crept like fog, dampening the light in his chest. He didn't know the precise rules, but he knew he wouldn't see much more of Charlise if her father didn't approve of him.

Charlise swirled, her blue skirt billowing, her laughter expanding and pealing across the ice, crisper than a church bell. Magic. The woman was magic, and he couldn't imagine a future that didn't encompass even a few minutes more of her time, her conversation, and her laughter. He'd noticed the trim of her clothes and knew his own were rough. He'd walked out with so little.

Sinclair made a mental count of the pay he had taken off the ship, and the extra coins he'd earned selling his syrups to Lawrence. Maybe, before that party, he should find a haberdasher and at least buy himself a new coat.

CHAPTER TEN

Charlise's thighs protested, and her cheeks were raw with cold. Her knuckles burned where the heat of her skin fought against the cold air.

Still, she skated.

Even after the Hempel children had left the ice and began to chase one another through the park. Neither did she stop when Elise, arms entwined with her new friend Rosanna, made her way to the edge of the pond. Charlise lunged and spun and stretched her arms as if she could go fast enough to fly, because for the first time in so long, she didn't feel scared or numb. She felt cold and sore and puffed and elated. She felt alive.

It was only when the grey turned inky that she finally relented to her body's pleas for rest, and reluctantly, she made her way to the end of the pond before clunking over the icy grass to rest on the bench. True to his word, Sinclair's knots were easy to untie. As she took the skates by the leather strap, the steel clinked like church bells. Charlise stilled them. She would not think about that today.

Sinclair had hung back, and while he tried to look busy in helping the Hempel's nanny line up the children, the occasional coy look tossed her way sent warm bursts of guilty delight through her. She fell into step beside him, the two of them bringing up the rear of the little line of cold and damp Honeysuckle Street children as they filed their way towards their homes.

'Within three days you've ensconced yourself in the street,' she said, somewhat incredulous. 'How do you do it?'

'It wasn't intentional.' He took a thoughtful breath. 'But my dad always says, there's something about a good drink that brings people together. Sweet, bitter, loaded, or temperate, it doesn't matter. People appreciate a thirst quenched, or an ache eased. When I started on the ship, I tried to prove myself with work and bluster, but I couldn't move fast enough, and I wasn't as strong as the others. But when a man has got a sore head from too much rum, and a bit of syrup eases it, well, let's just say that next time you struggle with a knot, instead of jeering, he'll take the time to show you how it goes.'

'We tasted your cordial last night. Aunt Petunia thinks you brought it for her, and I didn't say I thought it was for me.' She waited for him to correct her assumption, her heart spinning when he didn't. 'Sweet and tangy, refreshing and warming all at once. I've never tasted anything like it. I would have sent a note, but that is not appropriate. Last night, I decided to use my wish. And I wished I could see you and tell you. And now my wish has come true.'

'That's a very mundane thing to use a wish for,' he said.

'Sometimes, the small things are the best.'

They walked in companionable silence until, at the edge of the park, the children all scuttled across the granite, but when Sinclair stalled to wait for a slowly approaching carriage, Charlise paused with him. The light hung on the precipice between day and night, the eerie glow of evening when the sun had set but the gas lamps had not yet been lit, and normally exposed spaces became pockets of protective shadow. The road loomed like a line between the freedom of her day and her restricted reality, and she cringed at the thought of crossing back into that world.

'You skate like you're flying. I could have watched you all day,' he said.

'You are reprehensible. You cannot—'

'Help me with my etiquette then.' He cut her off with a smirked response. 'What should I have said?'

She paused. 'You *could* have said, you skate well, Miss Hartright.'

He clapped his hands behind his back, a slight arrogance in his bow as he tilted in her direction. 'You skate well, Miss Hartright,' he said. 'Next question. If I were at a ball, how would I ask a lady to dance?'

'If you don't know the lady, you ask the ballroom manager to make an introduction. If you know her, you may approach her yourself. And if she is disposed, she will add your name to her dance card.'

'A dance card. I understand.' Only the barest remnants of daylight remained the light so low it was more imagination than her vision that filled in his features. 'Before we cross, I have one last question. What is the meaning of this?' He pulled a small sprig of mistletoe from his pocket and held it high over the space between them.

'You have not encountered mistletoe before?' she asked, her voice as low as the light.

'No,' he said solemnly, although the corner of his mouth twitched, and his eyes sparkled with mirth. 'I was wondering why it is pegged over so many doorways.'

'There's a tradition. If two people are caught beneath the mistletoe, they kiss.'

'Tradition. Like a rule, then?'

'I suppose. But you can't just steal a kiss.' Charlise said, a reprimanding hint to her tone, even as she took a small step into his shadow. 'You pluck a berry first. When all the berries are gone, no more kisses.'

He reached above her, slowly, his fingers slightly fumbling as he held her gaze. 'I pluck a berry?'

'Yes.'

'And then I can steal a kiss?'

This was more than defying etiquette or propriety. They had moved into dangerous territory. Her sensibilities, every memorised stanza of every book on deportment and a proper young lady's behaviour, all of them screamed, No, no kisses.

'Yes,' she whispered, so softly her breath barely misted at all. 'But you are only allowed one.'

'Only one? Then I will make it worth the price of a berry.'

Plump and soft, the lightest brush of his lips sent a burst of stardust through her, and like the stretched arms of a snowflake, the tingling spread to the top of her head, glimmered in the tips of her fingers and toes, and glowed in her torso. Against the ice and chill, he was a crackling fire, thick blankets, mulled wine, the type of warmth that she could never get enough of.

'You taste like cinnamon and apples,' he mumbled against her as his hand snaked around her waist. 'And citrus. Divine.'

He trailed the small of her back, along her spine, before his fingers burrowed into her hair—no doubt loosening her perfect bun, but how little she cared. His tongue flicked against the seam of her lips, and slowly, she parted them, savouring his intrusion before meeting his hesitant flick with her own. He was cranberries, smoke, and hazelnuts, rich with salt and oil, delicious and earthy. She relaxed into him, and tentatively walked her fingers beneath his waistcoat, and held him like he could one day be hers.

Cold cheeks, warm lips, her heart pounding at a frantic pace, the world dissolved to nothing but the tautness of his body beneath her fingers, the smell of him, all sugar and fresh linen. Cold air skirted her skin, its chill fingers tickling her nape and corralling her into his warmth. If she were a snowflake, he was the palm that caught her, and she gratefully melted into nothingness. He adjusted the angle of his head a little, moved his tongue a little deeper, and pulled her a little tighter.

They broke apart with a puff of mist as cold air replaced warm breath.

'I don't think there are any entries in the etiquette books on that,' he said, pressing his forehead against hers before stealing another kiss, now all lightness and chaste lips. 'I didn't know a kiss could feel like that.'

If only her life were her own, if only she was free to walk and sneak kisses and fall in love with a man like Sinclair. To not worry about reputation and rank. To have someone look at her the way he did, without judgement. She scrunched his shirt into her palms, not wanting to relinquish the glimmer of him, but knowing she must.

'Sinclair, I need to tell you something. I—'

'Charlise?' Aunt Petunia called, her voice ringing into the evening. 'Are you still out here?'

Had her aunt seen them? Panicked, Charlise darted across the street, past the other houses and up the front steps until she reached her aunt, who stood silhouetted in the doorway of Number 7.

'You shouldn't be on the street alone' she chided.

'I thought I saw that cat,' Charlise stammered, making a show of looking across the road to Number 6. 'I was trying to pet him.'

Charlise glanced back to the shadow, her heart guilt-ridden and heavy with unsaid things. As she climbed the stairs, a lick of panic raced through her at the thought that her aunt might have caught sight of Sinclair as he crossed the road and ascended the stairs of Number 1, but then she turned back to Charlise and beckoned her closer. 'Spencer can take care of himself. Now, come inside before you take cold. We are rehearsing, and your father wants to hear your solo.' She took hold of Charlise's elbow and tugged her through the door.

'Mr McIntyre!' As Charlise crossed the threshold into the flush warmth of her aunt's home, she heard the light call of Miss Abberton as she hailed from across the street. 'I sampled your excellent cordial today. How many bottles could you produce by the day after tomorrow?'

CHAPTER ELEVEN

Charlise followed the hubbub of noise down the stairs to the kitchen. She hadn't been inside Number 1 before, but as all the houses in the row were built on the same plan, she navigated her way with ease.

Earlier that morning, she'd told her father she felt a headache coming on and was going to rest. She told Elise she was going to sit in the courtyard and wanted to be alone, and then had told Aunt Petunia she was reading a delicious novel and planned on squirrelling herself into a quiet corner of the library. Finally, she had told Annabelle, the house mistress, that she was going to take a turn along the street to invigorate her constitution. All of them, perhaps thinking it the weight of a young woman on the verge of becoming a wife, had solemnly nodded and promised to give her space.

Then, she had thrown a grey cloak over her flannel and wool house dress and slipped out the back door. She kept close to the fence as she skirted the lane, then snuck through the stables, clipped over the courtyard, and into the back door of Number 1.

As Charlise descended into the kitchen, she was greeted with bright flashes of copper and heavily scented steam mixed with smoke. An indistinct shape moved frantically between the stove, to coal in a bucket by the door, then back. The solid wood bench in the room's centre had been piled high with citrus, bundles of herbs, and fresh blossoms, along with blocks of sugar loaf wrapped in brown paper. She coughed until her senses adjusted to the onslaught.

'Sinclair?' she blinked hard as her eyes adjusted to the haze. 'Are you in here?'

'Blimey, Charlise. What are you doing down here?' he called from somewhere by the stove.

'I was concerned. My aunt told me that Miss Abberton made a significant order, and you don't have premises, or any assistants.'

'I can manage.' He thrust a wooden spoon into a heavy pot and stirred, then squatted to load chunks of coal into the stove belly, before slamming it shut and twisting the handle closed. 'If I am to be a self-made man, I need to manage all of this, I need to—'

Charlise wove through the chaos and grasped Sinclair by the wrists, turning him to face her. A thin line of sweat raced across his forehead, and one eye twitched in anxious thought. 'Let me help.' She squeezed, and realising she held his bare hands within her own for the first time, ran her thumb over the creases, relishing the brush of his hard edges against her own softness. Slightly rough at the knuckles, with smooth manicured nails, he trembled with energy.

'I need to show them. I need to...' he stammered, his eyes flicking.

'We will,' she said, wiping the sweat from his brow and smoothing a straggly curl. 'I can stoke a fire. And stir a pot. What would help?'

He stayed tense, then nodded in thought, a broad grin cracking. 'The fire,' he said, gesturing at the bucket of coal by the door. 'Then, will you help me sieve this syrup?'

The heat, the smell, the pace of it—as Charlise worked, she buzzed with not only energy, but with purpose. She fell into Sinclair's directions, watching with fascination as he sniffed at a chunk of ginger before cutting off a segment for mincing, or the way he inhaled the aroma coming off a pot before suggesting another slice of orange, or how he crumbled a sliver of sugar onto the bench. They worked around each other with such rhythm that the kitchen could have been a ballroom, the recipes their choreography as they bumped, joined, and separated from one another with the same eloquence required for a waltz. The ingredients on the bench slowly dwindled, and the collection of bottles on the kitchen table swelled.

By late afternoon, her wrists ached, but she fortified herself and finished juicing an orange. When done, and with no other tasks, she sidled beside Sinclair who intently studied a brew on the stove. He had rolled his shirt sleeves to his elbows, and his slightly bronzed muscles strained against the fold. She forced herself to take a steady breath, even though inside she let her stomach flip. He had unfastened his top collar button too, and the V made by his dishevelment lured her gaze down to the slight tautness of his chest, visible through the thin linen, before being hidden beneath his navy waistcoat. He reached across to the spoon on the bench, exposing his soft inner forearm, and the flip turned to fire as she imagined trailing her fingertips over his skin. There was no harm in just enjoying his closeness, was there? No sin in inhaling the rugged man who smelt of sugar and work? And if she leant into him, just a little, so that her arm brushed against his, would it, in the end, matter so much?

He took the spoon from the pot, blew lightly over the rose red liquid, then presented it to her. 'What do you think?'

It must have been a new wooden spoon, as when she sipped at the edge, its roughness brushed her tongue. Flavour exploded, sweet and strong and balanced.

'It's delicious,' she said.

'I'll need a better verdict than that,' he said. 'What does it taste like?'

'Cloves? And maybe cinnamon?' She licked her lips, trying to catch more of the flavour. 'It's cosy and... happy. This may sound odd, but it tastes like Christmas.'

'I wasn't sure the flavours would work.' He grinned with unconcealed pride. 'I wanted it to taste like an English Christmas, the sort you know that is a novelty to me. I wanted it to taste like catching snowflakes.'

It took all her control not to dissolve like sugar in warm water. He had made her a cordial. Sweetness and spice, the sort that warmed one from the inside out on a cold day, the flavour enough to shake the chill from stiff fingers. To make one feel alive.

The gentle sounds of the kitchen rippled in accompaniment to her breath, at odds with the tension in her chest. The fire popped, and the lyrical bubbling of the concoction on the stove filled the silence, and as her tongue brushed against the wood again, Sinclair gave the smallest sigh. Like the night before, he watched her intently, his dark eyes sparkling. The sweetness of his lips, and the gentle pressure of his embrace, all flared in her memory, and she rose onto her tiptoes, seeking his lips and he met her with a humble lightness.

A busy kiss.

Domestic.

Homely.

A crisp hiss came from the pot on the stove, and Sinclair startled. 'More zest,' he called, grabbing the pot by its handles and giving it a robust shake before setting it on the plate again.

Charlise returned to the bench and hurriedly scraped a lemon over the grater, hissing as she caught her knuckles against the ridges. She pinched the skin against her mouth to hide the graze. 'Finished,' she called, stepping back from the bench.

In two quick steps, Sinclair crossed the kitchen, swept the rind into his palm, then returned to the stove to sprinkle the bright yellow flecks into the pot. Using a thick towel, he moved it to the wooden bench, then gave a heavy sigh.

'Just this one to cool,' he said, his voice thick with relief. 'Then, once it's bottled, we're done.' His smile morphed into a frown. 'You're bleeding?'

'Just a nick from the zester.' Charlise fumbled for her handkerchief. 'Only small. It's the juice that makes it sting.'

He'd crossed the small distance between them and drew her to the sink before she could wrap the cotton around her fingers.

'This will help it numb,' he said as he guided her hand into the bucket of cool water. He rubbed his thumb lightly over the small gouge. 'You were so...'

Her distorted reflection stared blankly up at her as she waited for the words she had heard half her life.

Beautiful. Graceful. Delightful.

'*Competent*,' he said before raising her hand from the cold. He grasped for a nearby towel and shook it before wrapping it around her hand. 'Have you cooked like this before? I'm sorry, I don't mean cook, of course you have. But it's different, working in a busy kitchen. It needs more than knowledge; it takes intuition and improvisation. You're a natural.' He rummaged through a shelf, pulled out two glasses, then handed one to her.

Charlise flexed her fingers through the towel. Already the pain was dissipating, but she felt giddy. Breakfast had been hours ago, and apart from the odd slice of fruit, she hadn't eaten all day. With the stillness of the room descending, and only the lazy pop and crackle from the oven filling the silence, the kitchen that had been a hive of energy and activity now felt dangerously slow and intimate.

'I should go.' Her words carried all her assertion, because nothing else did—not her tone, her body, or her mind. She wanted to stay here, in the warm cocoon of his kitchen, in his busyness, sharing his sense of purpose in the world. 'They'll be wondering where I am. And my feet ache.'

'Take a weight off.' He grasped her by the waist and lifted her to the bench. Charlise squawked, then laughed, her boots swinging in the air.

He lifted a rough wooden crate onto the bench beside her, the bottles clinking. Green, blue, and clear glass stoppered with light brown corks.

'These are recipes from home. This one I made on the ship.' He tapped at the cork of one bottle. 'Used fresh fruit and flowers from the market in Sydney. Would you like to try?' He unstoppered a bottle with a light pop, then tipped a little liquid into one of the glasses and passed it to her. The thick syrup, tinged orange, smelt of citrus and summer blossoms. 'You only need a little. Just enough to coat your lips.'

Charlise tipped the glass back, the liquid not oozing but flowing thicker than water. The burst of flavour that melted against her tongue made her think of summer days, not the summer just gone, but before, when she was younger, when her and Elise used to drink water from streams and make daisy chains.

'It tastes like sunshine.' She licked her lips, catching a little of the flavour that remained. 'Is this your recipe?'

He shook his head. 'This was my mother's creation. She has more skill with flavour than me. She says the secret is to find something bitter to counter the sugar. She says a little sour makes the sweet more special.' He turned his attention back to the bottles in the case, pulling out one halfway, then gently sliding it back. He retrieved another and inspected the handwritten label. 'Tell me a memory.'

'A happy memory?' They'd all been buried so deep.

'Doesn't have to be.' He tapped at his chest. 'Just something you feel here.'

Charlise closed her eyes and took a slow breath. The aroma of woodsmoke and fruit lingered, and she had to breathe through the jumble to settle her senses to retrieve something untainted. She trawled through the days at her lessons, of walking endless laps of the library with books perched on her head, of laced corsets, skin creams, and hair pulled so high and tight it brought tears to her eyes. Before, before, before...

'I woke up, one morning,' she said, her voice so quiet even she could barely hear it. 'Everyone was still asleep. It was late January. It had snowed overnight, and everything smelt so clean. And it was so quiet, not even my mind dared to whisper. I went outside to my mother's garden, and there, amongst the snow, a purple crocus that she had planted was starting to blossom. The sun came over the hill, and it started to snow, and I was shivering but also felt so warm inside. It felt like everything happening at once, and like nothing happening at all. I've never felt less important.' Charlise scrunched her hands in her skirts and pinched her eyes tighter. 'I felt free.'

'Keep your eyes closed.' Another pop as a flask unstoppered, followed by a glug. His finger, firm and a little rough, ran across her lips. 'Taste it,' he said, his voice a rumble.

Chapter Twelve

As Charlise flicked her tongue over her lips, Sinclair bit down a sigh. That soft pink flicker of heaven, delicately naïve yet still curious and expectant, as delectable as a whisp of scented steam off the stove. Ethereal, unholdable, yet nonetheless imprinted on him.

'It tastes like...' her tongue moved slow as it explored the remnants of flavour, leaving her lips rich and glossy. 'Like a lazy afternoon at the end of a warm day. Like the pit in your stomach when you've done something you shouldn't, but haven't been caught, and you can't tell if you feel elated or guilty.' She licked the spoon again, and this time, he knew he did groan. 'Like the warm sun on your body before dressing. Like a perfect flower stolen from—'

Sinclair lunged, and their mouths crashed together, their kiss instantly deep and passionate. No delicate exploration like the night before, when he had teased her mouth gentlemanly and courteously. Not now as he took hold of her waist and drew her closer, his mouth opening against hers. Charlise let out a sigh as her nails pressed sharp against his neck. How could so small an action, the slightest nip of pain, send such a heady wave of desire and energy coursing through him?

'You taste like berries plucked warm from the vine,' he breathed against her. 'And like the sunrise. What I would give to taste the rest of you.' He trailed kisses across her cheek before scraping her earlobe with his teeth. 'To undress and know every part of you. To catalogue your body with my tongue.' She whimpered, then fumbled at her top blouse button, and as she released each fastening, he continued his sampling of her, nibbling down her neck to the slight swell of her breasts. Roughly, he tugged her corset down and wrenched her chemise aside, the fabric pulling taunt as her breast slipped free.

'This is wicked,' she exhaled, but still arched towards him, presenting her light pink nipple, and groaning as he drew it into his mouth.

'Thoroughly,' he mumbled against her. 'Touch yourself,' he said, working his way back to her mouth. 'And then let me taste your fingers.'

Sinclair worked at the button on her waistband, then took her hand.

'Touch myself?' she asked. 'You mean, my privates?'

'Have you ever done that? Brought yourself pleasure with your fingers?'

Her hand scrunched into a claw as her breath raked. 'A proper lady does not do such things.'

'You have never touched between your thighs and thought of some young man you've seen in the park, or danced with?'

Charlise gave a stifled groan, her fingers trembling where he held them taut at her waist. She flexed, then relented in her resistance, letting him guide her hand under the waistband of her skirt, under her petticoats, to rest at the gap in her drawers.

'Sometimes. Last night, as I bathed, I thought of you.'

'Show me,' he growled. 'How you enjoy it. Show me how you stoke desire in yourself.'

Unfettered. The word barged into his brain as her façade softened, and beneath his palm, her fingers moved assuredly, and with a pang through his chest and to his stomach, hard need reverberated through him at her dexterity, at the slight tip of her head as she moaned. He inhaled, burrowed into her, to taste the dip behind her ear.

'You are sin.' Her husky voice ground against his cheek, her finger still flicking beneath his hand.

'There is no sin in knowing your own body.' Her breath caught as he scraped his teeth against her neck, dragged over the bump of her collarbone, and tasted the salty exertion lining the depression. 'Let me taste you.' He slid his hand beneath her skirt, down the length of her arm, until his finger slid beside hers, circling as he sought to learn the pace of her pleasure. Once he had taken up the steady stroking, she disentangled herself and plunged her fingers between his lips with ferocity, and he greedily inhaled them.

He couldn't tell what was better—the delicate warmth of her body as he stroked, or the salty mustiness on the tip of his tongue. He drew her finger into his mouth, biting at the soft scrawl of her print, languid in his sampling of the desire he licked from her skin. 'You taste like abandon. Like too much wine. Like eyes on the horizon.'

He could bury himself between her thighs, breathe only her energy, feast on her desire until she broke against him. He withdrew his hand, enjoying the whimper from her as he did so.

'Taste yourself,' his voice a rumble through his chest as he pressed his thumb to her lips. 'You are delectable.'

Her tongue slid over his skin, her dark eyes wide with a glimmering want as brilliant as the sun glinting off ice. Sinclair's cock throbbed hard, and he rubbed against her, then snatched his hand from her mouth and burrowed through her skirts, and thrust his fingers between her thighs again, forgetting the steady motion of before. Her sharp cry cut as he buried his fingers up to the knuckle, and she dissolved into a shudder that nearly brought him undone.

'Touch me. Please.' He worked at his buckle, then loosened his waistband. He grappled in his pocket for a handkerchief, for after three months at sea, and five days of this luscious woman in his brain, he knew he wouldn't last much more than a few strokes. Her hand wrapped around his cock.

'Like this?' she asked, before moaning deeper, her thighs widening. 'You are wicked, Sinclair. You will unravel me.'

With his free hand, Sinclair gripped Charlise's chin and drew her mouth to his. He drunk her breath, stroked her faster, and thrust against her grip. Tighter and tighter her body wound, thighs clenching, her body jerking against his. A gasp, then a cry tumbled out of her, an incandescent, lyrical exhalation, and little spasms fluttered against his fingertips as she ground her wetness against his palm. The gentle tremor of her release echoed against him, and before he could draw breath and kiss her again, his own climax waxed and consumed, and he evaporated its bliss, only barely remaining cognisant enough to press his kerchief to his knob to stop himself from spending over her dress.

Gasping, Charlise seemed to melt against him. A thin bead of sweat from her forehead wriggled free before trailing the side of her nose and dissipating with a soft sheen over her cheek.

Sinclair tucked himself back into his trousers and stuffed his kerchief into his pocket. 'I fear I have been reading the wrong etiquette books. Sweet mercy. That was extraordinary.' He buried his nose behind her ear, loose curls of hair tickling his cheek.

Charlise tightened her grip on his neck. 'Sinclair, will you promise me something?'

'Anything,' he said, pulling her closer.

'Forget me,' she whispered. 'Please, please forget me.'

His heart, still thumping hard, cried out at the suggestion. 'How could I?'

'My future is not my own. My father, he's already made plans, and I—'

Sinclair pressed a finger to her lips. 'I know I don't seem much. But I have plans, too. I'll make my name. Look at what we did today. I'll show him.' He pulled her from the bench and set her steady on the tiles before cupping her chin and stealing another kiss. 'I'll show everyone.'

CHAPTER THIRTEEN

Charlise scrunched the fine red silk of her dress in her palms, as if the fabric were a rope and she could grasp it tight enough to hoist herself out of the pit she found herself in. She looked out from behind the stage curtain into the duke's ballroom, where the guests sat in rows of plush red seats. How could one man know so many people?

'My darling, please. You will stain the thread with your sweaty palms. If you are nervous, just breathe, like this.'

Charlise turned to the woman beside her. She needed no introduction; this could only be Miss Odette Delaney. Tall, lithe, elegant, and confident, she spoke with a delicate French accent, and as Charlise watched, she placed two fingers on her lower torso and took a slow inhalation, rolled her shoulders, then released it, counting as she did so. 'Sometimes, the only thing is to breathe. You are scared, *non*?'

'I am always scared,' Charlise confessed. 'But tonight, especially so. I have never sung before a crowd without the choir before.' Not just singing, but in all her life, she had done so little alone. She had always had her mother or sister beside her and had always relished the companionship and sense of belonging they gave her. But after tonight, she wouldn't have either of them. This song felt like the opening to her own musicale, where she would perform from solo to solo, never again blending into the comradery of the ensemble.

'No one wants you to fail, my darling,' Miss Delaney said. 'Don't sing to the crowd. Find a smile and give it your song.'

Charlise scrunched her skirts, then tutted to herself. Had she stained them? Was her fear on display to everyone? She took a breath, and with her chin held as high as she could manage, she moved to the centre of the stage, her eyes ranging over the crowd.

'Find a smile,' she muttered to herself. 'A smile.'

Frescos of angels, flowers, and mythical scenes graced the ceiling, and windows twice her size let in flickers of stars and night. The parquetry floor glimmered with the flame of a thousand candles. Everything within her squirmed—her blood, her mind, her breath, all of them fighting for contentment. Everything around her was stunningly beautiful, but also alien, cold, and distant.

Her gaze picked over the audience. She looked for stretched lips, or a row of teeth behind a grin. But all she found was expectation. Judgement. Stoic expressions, half-turned lips. The baron, twitching eyes and an expression that hesitated somewhere between satisfaction and disappointment. Did no one in the room have a smile for her?

And then she saw one. At the back of the room, because of course, that's where he would be. His grin warm and his eyes sparkling like sun on snow. The one face she didn't want to see, and yet light flooded her being at seeing him.

Charlise nodded to the pianist. He began to play.

For six sweet days, Sinclair McIntyre had swooped into her life and brought her joy and purpose and laughter. And tomorrow, she would walk down the aisle, then be whisked off to the country, possibly to never feel such things again.

Just a week ago, the thought would have had no impact. But tonight, as she sang the first notes of her song to the only tenderness in the room, the thought of living without those small moments of happiness made her voice tremble.

For Elise, she reminded herself. *Always, everything, for Elise.*

As she sang, the weight of her soul, the promise of love, the thaw of the snowflake and the shrivelling of her fear, all of it filled the melody. Charlise took a breath, tied every feeling into a ball and stuffed it down, but then Sinclair's grin cracked into a smile as wide as a broadsheet, and with it everything roared into being again, the cacophony of it so loud that it nearly drowned out the piano. With a crash, she remembered days with her mother and her father laughing, the four of them together, happy, and whole. Of looking at fabrics for her debut, or planting flowers. Sinclair's mouth on hers, ice skating, warm cordial and a cold wind. Her old life jarred against the staleness of her reality, and she sang her pain and loss into the room, to the expectant faces, the gathered curtains, and the flickering candles, until, words exhausted, the last echoes bounced, then whispered through the hall. For a moment everyone seemed frozen, and among the shocked onlookers she couldn't see any smiles, not even Sinclair's.

Then the room ripped with applause and shouts, even a whistle.

She'd done it. Not just sung but sung well. She curtsied, then sped from the stage, gasping with the life bounding through her. She clasped a hand to her mouth, breathing into her own sweat, craving the stillness of the room at Aunt Petunia's. She needed space. She needed to compose herself. She needed to make herself numb.

Instead, she thumped against Sinclair's chest.

'You were tremendous,' he said, wrapping his arms around her and swirling her in a semicircle. He pressed his beautiful rough palms against her cheeks and tugged her close, planting his lips on hers. 'I have something to tell you.'

'Sinclair, you can't. Someone will see.'

He grasped her hand and led her into a shadow beside the stairs. 'When I delivered the cordial, I asked Miss Abberton if she knew of any available premises. I am looking at an inn tomorrow. She says it needs work, but I am not scared of that.' He searched her face, his grip tightening. 'I'm going to be a man of means. A businessman. And I know we've had a rather rushed start, but what's between us is something. I feel it, in every part of me. When we work in the kitchen. When we kiss. We're magic.'

His lips crashed into hers, warm, soft, delicate, and sweet. Beyond the encompassing comfort of his embrace, she faintly registered the dying applause, and a name being called. Her name. She jerked, then pulled back. Tears stung her eyes, and she pressed the back of her hand to her mouth, stifling a sob.

'I didn't mean for it to be like this, I swear.' He reached for her, and she stepped out of his reach. Why was a simple movement such agony?

'I don't understand.' Sinclair began to follow her.

'Charlise, my intended. Where are you?' The baron. He must have climbed onto the stage because he now stood central, peering into the stage curtains and frowning. 'I am trying to invite our new friends to our wedding.'

'Intended?' Sinclair pushed the curtain aside and stared out, his expression shifting from confusion to anger. 'The man from the park? You're engaged? To *him*?'

'Go,' she said, placing her hand on his chest and giving him an unconvincing shove. 'Please don't make a scene. I know I deserve it, but please, don't. For Elise.'

'Charlise...' the baron called again, now impatient. 'Now is not the time for games.'

Sinclair's nostrils flared as his hands bunched into fists by his side. Harsh words screamed in his eyes, and in them she saw every slanderous sentence and critical whisper ever muttered about her amplified.

'For Elise,' he squeezed out between gritted teeth. 'Go. Your baron is waiting.'

Since her ruination, she had known the cut of a turned back, but nothing had split her so painfully as Sinclair turning away, his eyes spitting venom, his lips curling in judgement.

Charlise took a breath, then exhaled.

One, two, three, four, five, six, seven.

Then she stepped onto the stage and took up the hand of the man who, in less than a day, would be her husband.

Chapter Fourteen

People didn't move out of Sinclair's way. They sidled. His angry exit was so inconsequential that not even a curious head bothered to turn to follow his step.

Applause, cheers, notes, all of it spewed forth from the damn duke's residence, and Sinclair gratefully put it behind him with each step as he descended from the tenth house in the street to the familiar shadow of Number 1. He wrenched the door open and staggered into the entry before slamming it behind him. As he tugged off his coat, his bloody brand-new coat, and slammed it into the tiled floor, he caught sight of three pairs of eyes in the front parlour that leant forward in their seats to watch him, intently.

Phineas, Felix, and a new face.

'McIntyre.' Phineas gestured at a crystal carafe on a small table beside him. 'Can I get you a drink?'

'I don't drink,' Sinclair replied.

'Tonight, you do.' Phineas sloshed clear liquid into a glass and held it out.

Sinclair took the glass from Phineas, then sniffed. Gin. A drink for misery if ever there was one. He tipped back the contents in one gulp, coughing a little, but forced himself to stifle it as he savoured the hot burn against the cold hurt in his chest.

'Who are you?' Sinclair gruffed at the newcomer.

The new face raised an eyebrow. 'Arley.'

'You're missing that fancy party, Arley.' Sinclair snapped, knowing he was being rude, but his indignity pushed out any thought of etiquette or even basic manners. 'At that blasted duke's house. Don't you want to be there, hobnobbing with all the toffs? Why are all of you here?'

A look he couldn't decipher passed between the three of them. After a long silence, Arley spoke. 'I'm not one for parties,' he said before taking a sip of his gin. 'Especially ones at dukes' houses.'

'And Christmas makes me maudlin.' Phineas, slightly swaying, stood, then refilled Sinclair's glass. He nodded at the vacant chair. 'Sit,' he said before slumping back into his own seat.

'I don't feel like talking,' Sinclair grumbled as he sunk into the chair.

'Then don't,' Arley said.

Sinclair ran his fingers over the delicate finesse of his glass. Made from fine cut crystal, it was likely worth more than his every possession.

'A baron,' he muttered, then took another sip. 'All this time, engaged to a goddam baron. And he is rubbish with his horse. And he's so...' Sinclair threw his hands into the air, lacking the proper words to expel his disgust, then took swig of gin. 'I could have given her... given her...' What, exactly, could he have offered? A promise of a future? He didn't have one to give. His heart? Useless, thumping thing that it was, circulating the ancestry of convicts and workers.

The only thing this city loved more than money was blood, and he had neither.

''Tis better to have loved and lost...' Phineas spun one hand in an elegant circle, before pausing, suspended and lost. He stared into the fire before his gaze drifted to the mantle, before settling on a framed photograph of a straight-lipped sepia woman. He took another hefty sip. 'Apparently.'

'Who's the woman?' Sinclair asked.

Phineas topped up his drink. 'I thought you didn't feel like talking,' he said, then sunk back into the chair, resting his glass on his chest.

Sinclair took a measured sip. He actually did feel like talking, but as he looked at the three men, he could tell there'd be no comfort in any unburdening of anger, only a deepening of grief. They all had a look of dark absence about them, the company of others not filling a void, only creating a buffer to ensure their own malady didn't expand and smother. Instead, he stared into the flames.

Sometime after the third log placed by Felix had dissolved into ash, Arley left, and when both Phineas and Felix gave rumbling snores, Sinclair slipped up to his room. When he finally reached the fourth-floor landing, he crossed the short distance to his door with a heavy step. He slid his hand across the wooden panel, lowering his candle to find the handle wrenching it down and stepping inside.

'What are you doing here?' He should have felt some surprise at seeing Charlise sitting on his bed, still wearing the bright red gown from the party, its hem stained dark with thawed sleet, but the gin had numbed his edges and forced out any emotion other than indignation. 'Don't you have duties to attend to. Etiquette to follow. Baroness.' He hissed the last word, and she shied like she'd been struck.

'I wanted to explain,' she said, not looking up from her entwined fingers in her lap.

'I already know. It's right here in your blasted book.' He crossed the room and dropped the brass candle holder onto his bedside table before snatching up the etiquette guide and flicking through the pages. *Beware of some coquette, some "lady of unmeaning attentions" who is only anxious to behold lovers in her train—'*

'Six days and you have deciphered this city?' She cut him off with a half-choked sob, quiet anger flashing across her face. 'How delightful for you to know everything. To be able to choose how you roll your dice, to act rashly and still land on your feet like a cat.'

'But why *him*?' Sinclair half shouted, flinging his hand in the vague direction of the higher numbers of the street.

'Because he's the only man that would have me!' Charlise rose, her voice tangled and pinched with anguish. 'I am ruined. And not a little. Properly. Completely. Everyone knows. Marrying restores a little of my reputation, and with it, Elise. She doesn't have a chance otherwise.' Wind whispered at the window sash, and a few heavy drops of rain splatted loud against the glass. 'I should have told you. But for the first time in so long, someone wasn't judging me. I just wanted to hold that feeling for the smallest sliver of time.'

A slip of breeze squeezed between a gap in the window sash, but that wasn't why he felt cold and sick inside. Shame, as heavy as ice, spread through him. At the first moment of being tested, he'd failed, leaping to judge in as hurtful a way as he could, thinking words he'd promised his grandmother he would never fling at a woman.

'It began with Mother.' She huffed a small laugh, and in it, he could hear the threads of a beautiful yet painful memory. 'Everything always did. Her father had been a lesser son of an earl. Father is the third son of a captain in the dragoons. The right blood, but just born in the wrong order. She'd tell us stories about what life was like at her uncle's house, and we'd dream of marrying princes. She spent hours planning my debut. I was going to be presented to the queen at court. It was going to be perfect. And then, she got sick.'

Sinclair sat on the bed and placed his hand over Charlise's fidgeting fingers and squeezed them gently until they stilled.

'She was in such pain, and for so long,' she continued, every word a labour, as if the weight of the memory slowed them. 'Father called every doctor, prayed constantly at her side, but nothing helped. They hadn't been a love match, but they grew into each other, and when she was gone, grief swallowed him. We stayed in full mourning for more than a year. When I think of those days, I don't even remember them as having any colour in them. That was, until Benjamin.'

Sinclair tampered down the unwelcome flick of jealousy at the mention of another man's name, and instead, stroked her palm with his thumb.

'He was a labourer's son who helped in the garden. He'd worked alongside my mother, and after she was gone, I tried to take her place. We talked as we planted seeds or pulled weeds. One day, he kissed me.' A dimple indented her cheek, and he could see the simplicity of the memory, and the innocence of the moment. She took a determined breath, then swallowed. 'And then we kissed a little more. And then *did* a little more. I'd hurt for so long, only known black and the sad ritual of loss. And it all felt so *good*.'

Little wonder she'd curved into him, spread so beautifully, kissed so deeply. Her body craved gentleness and love, as if dehydrated. The innocent smile turned to torment, and she hunched her shoulders again.

'He told his friends. And in a heartbeat, I was the gossip of the village. And my father, he wasn't angry or mad. He blamed himself, adamant that he'd failed my mother. He had two daughters he'd promised to marry well, and now we were both tainted. He said we had to restore the family name. Not only for me, but for Elise.'

Sinclair tugged at one of the wool blankets bunched at the end of his bed and draped it over her shoulders. 'The baron—it doesn't bother him?' he asked as he tucked the soft wool around her. 'That you're not—'

'Oh, it bothers him.' She cut him off with that same fire from before, anger flashing between the cracks in her proper façade. 'He has negotiated additional compensation in my dowry. He reminds me constantly. I am sure on our wedding night he will remind me still.' She shuddered, as if already wanting to shake off the man's touch. 'And I had stuffed everything down, ready to atone for my sins and accept my fate. Until you.' Her tone turned bitter as a lonely tear streaked her cheek, its trail luminescent in the candlelight. 'You made me remember snowflakes and skating and berries and cold air. I was a young woman again. And I've tried to smother it all, but I can't.' She turned into him, pressing her forehead to his chest, and he wrapped both arms around her. 'You need to erase me,' she whispered. 'I will not be able to bear my life otherwise.'

'Erase you?'

'Use me. Do anything you like with me. Teach me a lesson for how I treated you. For leading you on. I am already ruined.' She gripped his shirt at the waist, like she had when they kissed, her fists pushing against his hips. 'Break me, Sinclair. I want you to obliterate me.'

In the dark recesses of his mind, he knew what she was asking. To be bent as suited him, to be used hard, for him to treat her as nothing more than a beautiful body existing only for his pleasure. For him to shake all the gentleness of the past few days and cover them with a selfish memory, where her only purpose was his satisfaction. To knock her from the pedestal he had placed her on and leave her whimpering on the floor when he was done.

'I can't do that,' he whispered, stroking the soft skin behind her ears. He breathed her, her melancholy, her freshness, her dashed hopes. 'I don't have it in me.' A lie as filthy as the sordid images in his mind, because if he gave his lust and pride free rein, he could do all she asked of him and more. She twisted out of his embrace with a sob, but he held her firm. 'But I'll not leave you for him to break. Stay. Stay the night, and I will make you indestructible.'

Chapter Fifteen

Charlise's breath rasped as she nestled against the fold of his shirt collar, soft from wear. The tight pull of her hair eased a little as he removed a hairpin and set it on the bedside table.

'You are no hellion. No grand seducer. *Fallen.*' He chuckled, and the little huffs of his breath caressed her nape. 'One groping afternoon does not diminish you.' Another pin removed, then another, and her combs. An uneven lock fell across her shoulder before all her curls tumbled. He tickled his fingers through the lengths until they loosened, and every hair on her head prickled, every bump, every pore suddenly enraptured and stimulated. 'But you must promise me that you will never, ever, draw the memory of me into your mind when he is with you. I'll not keep the same bed as that man. This is only for you. For mornings when you wake early and reach for that place between your thighs. Or perhaps, when you bathe, surrounded by steam and hot water, and you let the water trickle through your delicate creases. Remember me. And one day, when you find yourself free, use this memory to rebuild all the broken pieces. Remember who you are right now and make yourself whole.'

Charlise swayed, already about to crumple into him, thoughts crashing like waves against a hull in confusion as she tried to imagine how a memory might fulfil such a monumental task.

'Do you promise me?' he asked.

With each unfastened bodice button, Sinclair planted a kiss on her exposed skin, until he reached the curve of her breasts that showed above her corset and chemise. His fingers so nimble, so lithe, continued to work, while his breath, his tongue, his lips tickled. Her skin seared, her body already aching.

'I will do anything you say,' she said.

'No,' he said, his mouth branding the word onto her skin. 'You will tell me what to do.'

'But I don't know anything. Apart from that once, I don't know—' her heart started its familiar, anxious flutter.

His laugh, light and soothing, cut her off. 'Yes, you do. It's all in here.' He pressed his palm against the stiffness of her corset, over her thumping heart. 'You just need to give yourself permission. Tell me what you like.'

Her bodice unfastened, she relaxed her arms in surrender. Sinclair tugged it loose and cast it aside, but he made no move to undress her further, only drew patterns on her body. Eyes closed, she thought of the rush of the past few days. The moments that had sent her heart lumbering and turned her knees into syrup. 'I like your mouth,' she whispered. The phrase felt inadequate and innocent, but then, she was, wasn't she? Hadn't he recognised her for what she felt herself to be—a naïve woman who had fallen into a feeling?

He laughed again, this time a little more wicked. 'So, when I...?' His tongue finished the question, his lips pressing into the cavity behind her ear. His breath trickled over her, oozing through her body and banishing the chill.

'I feel that all over. I tingle everywhere.' She let the warmth bubble and permeate. He worked at her skirt, and she reached to help him with the fastenings. As soon as they were loose, before her skirt had slipped even a little, she began to work at her petticoat ties, and the ribbon of her bustle.

'Where would you like my mouth now?' he asked.

'On—' Charlise bit her lip. 'On my...'

'Say it,' he growled.

'Would you kiss my breasts?' she asked, then hid her face against his shirt.

He chuckled, his voice humming over her skin. 'I will kiss you everywhere.'

Her words devolved into a gasp as he gripped her bottom tight, his fingers digging into her flesh in rough possessiveness as he pulled her against him. She tugged at his tie, and he fumbled then pulled it loose before he grabbed her by the waist and raised her, her boots kicking free of the weight of her skirts as they pushed them to the floor, and giggling, they fell back against the bed.

Charlise collapsed into the soft pillows and sheets, and the scent of him, all soft leather, sugar, and spice rose around her. Then he was upon her, his lips hard against hers, eager and demanding. He grasped her hands and pushed them into the mattress, slid them over her head and held them there, all while she drank his kisses, met his tongue, and when she had opportunity, the salty lust from his neck.

'My boots,' she said, arching with a moan as he rubbed his hardness against her. It seemed unfair that her body was exposed and vulnerable to him through the gap in her drawers, while he remained hidden. 'And why are you still dressed? I want to see you.'

'One thing at a time,' he tutted before pushing himself back on his haunches. 'You have no idea how magnificent you are. Charlise, you are—' She let her knees fall wider and arched her back, instinct more than knowledge guiding her. Kneeling, he tilted his head to one side, his tongue flicking between his lips. 'Amazing. Everything about you.'

He settled back on his heels and raised her ankle, pressing the sole of her boot to his chest. 'Your strength.' He flicked the loop from one button free, his strong fingers not needing a boot hook, and as she remembered the skill of those same fingers she thrust towards him, her body seeking contact but finding only air. 'Your wit.' Another button, and another. 'Your vitality.'

Flick, flick, each button came free, and he wiggled her boot loose then lowered her stockinged foot to the bed.

'You like my mouth?' he asked.

She nodded. 'So much.'

He smirked, wicked and wild. 'Even though I am uncouth. Improper. And never say the right thing?'

'Especially then.' She writhed in anticipation.

'Good.'

Confusion rose as he half disappeared from her view, only the curve of his back and his waistcoat buckle visible. And then his mouth, his mouth, began to work against her. His tongued tickled, then gave a slow, gentle sweep, until, goodness, she'd only ever been told to call her body there her privates, but with Sinclair's mouth pushed hard against her, his tongue plunging *inside* her, they had become anything but private. The gates that surrounded her world seemed to creak open even as she widened for him. She gripped the sheet and moaned, her thighs clenching, her body desperate.

He sat up, then casually raised her other still booted foot to his chest. 'You are the most sumptuous thing I have ever tasted. You are better than honey laced with cinnamon. Chocolate and salt.' As if seeking inspiration for a compliment, he bent again, and Charlise jerked as his tongue skimmed her, slow and lapping.

She felt knotted with desire, craving a fulfilment she could not ever remember needing before, seeking the unimaginable. With Benjamin, she'd felt a flicker of enjoyment and a light relief before the pain of his coupling, and her confusion about his arhythmic movements, his grunting before a final collapse against her. It hadn't felt bad, but compared to the tremors Sinclair ground through her, it could have been nothing more than a sneaky sip of port, or a stolen sweet.

Sinclair's breath ran warm through the cotton over her thigh before moving lower, over her knee and down her calf, to the place above her boot where he'd stroked her skin. Another dexterous unbuttoning followed by a wiggle and her boot dropped to the floor.

'I want to see you,' she rasped, breathy and demanding.

He sat back on the bed and stretched his arms, palms exposed. 'Do what you will.'

As Charlise caught her breath, he sat motionless, and it took her a moment to realise that he was waiting for her. She tucked her calves beneath her and shuffled closer, so that their knees touched, then rose until they were almost the same height, practically equal. As she fumbled with his waistcoat and shirt buttons, Sinclair pulled at her corset tie, the rubbing of the cord its own breath.

'Just as you are right now. There is a memory to last me a lifetime,' he said.

'Do I look pleasing,' she asked, kissing the dip at the base of his neck as she exposed it, flicking her tongue in imitation of his kisses on her. 'Poised?' Further down she moved, over his heart, and against her open mouth it thudded, strong and frenetic. 'As a young lady should?' She untucked his shirt, and he helped her strip it and his undershirt from his body, then threw the lot into a jumble on the floor.

'Truth be, you look frightful. Your hair is a mess. You are completely dishevelled.' He fumbled with her corset hooks, frowning. Charlise grasped the edges, and with a practised flick, pulled them open. Sinclair helped lift it over her head, then her chemise, and the chill of the room sent a shiver over her nakedness. 'But your confidence. That's the memory I'll take with me. Hold that feeling. Remember it, always.'

And she felt it. Felt self-assured, even though she had never been more exposed to another person, never been more unsure of what she was doing. With him, she could have faced lions, or sung an aria at Covent Garden. Hungry for his kisses, for his rough hands, she pulled him closer, and he quickly responded, working at his trouser fastening, kicking them off, his shoes thumping to the floor, and then he was tugging at her drawers, and she lay back against the pillows as he levered her free.

He toyed with her stocking ribbons, tied in a bow just above her knees. 'I could leave these,' he said with a slight growl. 'You look thoroughly naughty. Completely improper.'

'All of it,' she said, and he groaned a little as she widened her thighs. 'I want to be completely exposed.'

With an exaggerated sigh that made her giggle, he untied the bows and tugged her silks by the toes until they flicked free. He slid his hands along her naked calves, her thighs, then stroked between them.

Like a tight string released, pleasure, warmth, and tingling ecstasy rushed through her as he slipped his fingers into her, his thumb circling her nub as the melody of his movements rose into a crescendo. Her body swimming with bliss, she managed to prise her eyes open and take in his naked form. The light fuzz of hair over his hard chest, gathered to a delicate line that trailed down his abdomen, leading to the most delicious looking arrow where his torso met his thighs, his skin smooth and lean, and his manhood, heavens. Charlise looked away, knowing she was blushing, even as Sinclair stroked her faster, and she cried out with the heavenly sensation of his strokes.

'You can look,' he said, straightening in invitation. 'I would enjoy you looking at my cock.'

'It's much bigger than Benjamin's,' she blurted, before covering her mouth in embarrassment, half closing her knees in shame. Surely it was crass to make such a comparison in bed.

Sinclair withdrew his fingers, and Charlise thought he was stopping because he was angry with her, but when she found courage to look up at him, he was grinning mischievously. 'I don't think that matters all that much, especially if a man is not going to pay attention to a lady's needs.' He put his index finger to his lips and licked, his eyelids fluttering as he groaned. 'A flavour that cannot be bottled. What a delicacy you are.'

'Sinclair, I want your...' she took a breath, stealing herself. 'I want your cock,' she whispered.

He kissed her neck, then drew a nipple into his mouth and circled his tongue over its point. 'How?' he murmured against her, his growl rumbling.

'I want it in my... in my...'

'Your thatch? Your pussy? Your cunny?' He pressed his lips to her ear, then growled, 'Your cunt?'

'In my...' He'd given her too many words, too much new information, and she clutched at what to say. 'In my privates,' she stammered.

His laugh, soft, rich, warm as mulled wine and just as spicy, rolled over her. He laid a hand on her cheek and drew her close. He tasted musky, smelt of desire, and he kissed her with the same domestic lightness as he had in the kitchen, and her heart lurched for a time, a place, a future where he would plant kisses like that, not in secret, but in a living room at the end of a long day, or in the morning before he took himself off to his employment. 'Even when you are trying to be wicked, you are still so sweet.' He stretched beside her, pushing himself up. 'Sit astride me, then wrap your legs around me.'

Charlise slid her thighs either side of his and wrapped her arms around his shoulders, before running her fingers through his slightly knotted hair. He held her torso as she encircled him, hooking her knees about his waist and letting her ankles cross at the small of his back. He took his privates—no, his cock—and angled himself towards her body, and with a smooth plunge, pulled her down and buried himself in her.

'Oh, heavens,' were the only words she could utter as he filled her, so sure and satisfactory, and if anything she had felt before was good, this was akin to bliss, sweet, oblivion, even better that his fingers in the kitchen, than his mouth. His firmness sent a spasm of pleasure through her so indescribable all she could do was clutch a handful of his hair, and tense her entire body against his. Sinclair too gasped, arched, and wrapped his arms around her, clutching her tighter and moving deeper.

Thrusting, kissing, grabbing, and moaning, Charlise let his body dictate to hers. When he rose, she widened her thighs, and when he moaned, she inhaled, drank him, and kissed his mouth and neck, before licking the tang from his clavicle and running her teeth over his ear lobe. In response, he pinched her nipples so that a jolt of pain ran through her, but in the same instance, it amplified every tingling nerve of pleasure and rabid ecstasy. But it wasn't enough, she wanted more, not the slow measured movements that were restricted by their entanglement, the delicate patience of each thrust, and the light caress of his fingers. She needed to unhinge him.

'Deeper, Sinclair,' she dug her heels into his back. 'I need all of you.'

'I don't want to hurt you.' He buried his face against her shoulder. 'You are so innocent. So—'

She grasped his hair and pulled his face close to hers. 'I am not innocent. I am ruined. Not because of before. Because of you. I am yours, Sinclair.' Then she kissed him hard, as hard as the need coursing through her, as hard as the thumping of the blood in her ears. She was desperate for release, for satisfaction, and for freedom. 'I am lost to you. I want to see you lose yourself in me.'

For a moment, he faltered, and uncertainty flashed in his eyes. Charlise arched her body, tensed her thighs, and pulled herself tighter against him, forcing herself upwards, pulsing along his shaft and presenting her nipple, which he greedily took into his mouth with an emphatic grunt. Then his whimper turned into a roar, and with a dizzying swiftness, he wrapped his arms around her and flipped her, plunging her deep into the feathered mattress, crumpling her into the soft pillows as he thrust his cock hard into her.

'Is that what you want? All of me?' he grunted, each word punctuated with a slap of his thighs against hers.

She wailed with pleasure, lost as his lean hips rubbed hard against hers, his torso slippery with sweat. Her thighs stretched and burned as he pushed his weight against her, all of her senses singing in a phrenzy of abandon. She felt him in every nerve and breath and pulse.

'Yes, yes, yes,' she sang, not caring if anyone heard her, hoping that her euphoria echoed loud enough to shatter every damn rule that this city placed before her. In a crescendo, her body arced, thrummed, and hesitated as if suspended over a precipice, then swooped so hard and fast and headlong into the most mind-boggling ecstasy it blotted out sight and breath, her every sense lost in the terrific energy of it. Completely untethered, she relented, even as he pressed himself deeper, grunting, groaning in his own bliss, his moans sending ripples over her skin. His weight morphed from heightened to relaxed, from wrought to liberated, from tight within himself to dissolving. Charlise captured his body against hers, tighter, and held him, waiting for an end she couldn't predict, but knowing that every small tremor was a moment with him she wanted to hold tight in her memory, in her person, in her soul.

Eventually, cold nipped at her toes and her fingertips. Sinclair rolled to lie alongside her and pulled her close against his chest. Although she felt the most immense satisfaction, she still felt the loss of him. Already, the magic of the moment was leaving her, and no amount of clamouring would draw it back. Time moved relentlessly on.

He sighed, breathy and satisfied. 'I am absolutely ruined.'

'You will forget me,' she said, even as she snuggled into his chest, enjoying the weight of his arm as it draped across her. 'You will find another woman to give you pleasure. It is the way of all men.'

'Never,' he said. 'I'll not lie, I am no innocent. But that's why I know that finding satisfaction elsewhere will be pointless. No one will compare with you. Nothing, ever and forever. Since I saw you sing, all I could think of was how to claim you, how to make you mine. And now, the opposite is true. I am not one for poems or devotions or lyrics, but my simple honesty is in my every fibre. The places where your body touches mine feel alive, and when you leave, they will ache. I am yours forever, and I give myself freely. You came here to destroy yourself, but my lovely Charlise, you have destroyed me.'

She wanted to protest and tell him that men were not built that way, but even as she drew breath, he stroked her waist and gathered her tighter, and with a sigh, she found the rise of his chest, rested her cheek against it, and let herself fall. 'I should go,' she said, hating the words even as her breath gave them voice. 'They cannot find me here.'

'Sleep,' he said. 'I'll wake you before the window knockers are rousing. Let's pretend that this is what it's like for us, even though it's not.'

'You'll wake me?'

'I sat watch over the ship for many a night. Tonight, I'll watch over you.'

It felt dangerous to trust him. But still, she did. As he tucked the blankets around them, she let the dim warmth of dreams encapsulate her in their cloak, her mind drifting to sleep to a new song: his breath the bass, his heart the rhythm, her pulse the melody, two bodies singing like a symphony.

He nudged her awake before the robins chirped, helped her dress, walked her three doors down, and released her to the shadow of Number 7.

Just as he had promised he would.

Chapter Sixteen

Sinclair checked the time. Three minutes past ten. Abberton was only a few minutes late, but inactivity made him restless at most times, and this morning, he felt fragmented, and even a minor frustration threatened to shatter him.

Was she married? Had she said I do? Was she no longer Miss Hartright, but that awful man's baroness?

The little inn he sat outside was located in a district that seemed poised on change. The building itself looked determinedly shabby, but its neighbours—a coffeehouse and a draper—both had fresh paint, and the little rectangle windows that made up each shopfront were clean, with no soot collecting along their edges. A weak sun glinted off whole panes of glass hidden behind wooden shutters, all of which needed painting, but the stone façade looked solid, as did the thick wooden mantle over the door. Even with flaking paint, the building had an air of contentment.

Sinclair, now agitated, tapped his crate with his foot. He'd left a bottle in the kitchen of Number 1 as thanks for Phineas's hospitality. He would have thanked him personally, but as he left with his duffle bag on his back, his host still snored in his chair in the parlour. Phineas's generosity had never been endless. And, at days end, he couldn't imagine climbing into a bed that smelt of Charlise, where the only images he would see would be of her liberated naked body writhing beneath his, all while knowing she was another man's wife.

Besides, it was time for Sinclair to make his own way. And securing this inn was his first, proper step on his path to becoming a self-made man.

Well, if Abberton ever turned up it would be.

Surely a little peak wouldn't hurt?

Inside, Sinclair coughed into his shirt sleeve as particles that hadn't moved in years floated into orbit. Miss Abberton hadn't been lying when she said the place had good bones but needed work. Thick dust lined each surface, and like outside, paint flaked and curled. But the wooden beams overhead ran straight, the bench that ran the length of the room knocked solid when he thumped it, and although he trod gingerly at first, the floor did not ease or creak beneath his feet. He slid his crate onto the bench and the bottles clinked in their familiar melody.

'Good bones.' The deep, forthright voice came from the door. Sinclair spun to meet it. Tall, dressed in an immaculate black suit, with grey flecked hair and bright blue eyes that sparkled, the stalwart man in the doorway could only be Albert Abberton.

'Sir,' Sinclair crossed the room in a few eager strides. Abberton had an even shake, the press of a man content with his place in the world. 'The building is beautiful. How has it been empty for so long?'

'It was received as payment for a deal gone bad, and then promptly forgotten about,' he said as he tucked his top hat under his arm.

'And then you bought it?'

Abberton barked a laugh. 'No, dear boy. The man who forgot about it is me. Thank heavens Iris spotted the paperwork, hey?' He leant against the bench and peered into Sinclair's crate. 'I find business goes better over a drink. Any sherbets in there? Something we don't have to mix?'

'A couple.' Sinclair pulled out a bottle and two short glasses, before setting them on the bench and filling them. He slid one across.

Abberton took a sip, then closed his eyes, clearly savouring the flavour. 'That is something, even without a dram of brandy to make it kick. You have a talent, that's for certain.' He rolled the glass between his fingers. 'Before we talk terms, tell me why you want this.'

'I've always been in everyone's shadow; my brothers', my father's.' As Sinclair spoke, pride, relief, and anticipation rushed through him, enthusiasm blossoming in his chest. 'I think there's a time for a man to stand on his own skill, and that's what I want. To make my own way. Make my name. Become a self-made man.'

Abberton nodded thoughtfully, then took another sip. 'Forgive my crassness, but that's the biggest pile of horseshit I've ever heard, and I can tell you, in my work, I hear quite a bit.'

Sinclair mouthed a protest, gawping soundlessly, until his confusion found voice. 'But you're one of the most accomplished men in London. Even my father spoke of you, and the business you built.'

'I'm not saying there's nothing in a name, because there's plenty, especially in this city. But without my darling daughter, without the friends who filled the duke's hall last night, without the men who sweat and labour for me and go home with a decent wage in their pocket, do you think all that effort is worthwhile? Life isn't about work or achievement. It's about the spaces in-between. To love is to live, my boy. If you can't build a future around others, you may as well tip this elixir into the Thames and be done with it.'

Loneliness seeped into him as he absorbed Abberton's words. He'd wailed and blustered against his family, desperate to be seen, never quite able to step back and appreciate himself as part of an interconnected web, as a cog in something bigger. One ingredient in a recipe. One set of hands in a production line. A note in a song. A voice in a choir.

'Despite that,' Abberton continued. 'You are in luck, for I am a ridiculously sentimental old man, especially at Christmas, and I'd love to see this place cleaned up. How does this sound for terms: first year's lease, I'll take a crate of this a week. The place doesn't need much by way of materials, but it does need time and grit.'

Sinclair's mind bounded as it absorbed the ludicrously good offer Abberton had just made him, but somehow, an agreement didn't spring to his lips.

Abberton took the bottle and topped up his glass. 'I think this one is my favourite,' he said, holding it up to the light. A ray of sun glinted through the window, then the glass, casting a crimson triangle onto the bench.

'Charlise—I mean, Miss Hartright—she likes that one too.' Sinclair's voice rasped, the catch in his throat more pronounced than he would have liked.

'Miss Hartright? That lovely girl who is to become my new neighbour? She has a trial ahead of her. That house does not have solid beams like this place. I can't imagine she'll be comfortable there.'

Sinclair stared out the window at the thick slats of the shutters. 'I can't imagine she will be,' he said.

'The baron is ambitious, though. He wants to conquer the world, but I'm not sure he has the makings of a good husband.' Abberton shook his head. 'It's one thing for a man to decide he'll disagree with his family. But it's a much harder task for a woman, at least not without consequences. Alone, choosing her own path is practically impossible.'

I think you are quite brave to try and stand on your own, Charlise had said. But he hadn't, not in earnest, even when he imagined himself making a break. Friedrich had given him a chance and taken the time to teach him the ropes. Phineas had provided him with a room and a kitchen. Lawrence had given him encouragement when he felt most desperate. And Miss Abberton had made her order and recommended this place to him. So many small gestures helping him move forward. But who was there to help Charlise?

'What church?' Sinclair snapped, urgency rising in him. Abberton startled. 'The wedding, Charlise and the baron. What church is it at?'

'In the little chapel by the park at the end of Honeysuckle Street.' Abberton took out his pocket watch and clipped it open. 'Ceremony must be about to start.'

Maybe, just maybe, he'd have time. 'I'm sorry, Mr Abberton, but I'm going to have to turn down your generous offer.' He slung his duffle over his shoulder, dodging upturned chairs as he made for the door. 'Keep the cordial,' he called over his shoulder. 'As thanks for your trouble.'

Months before, Sinclair had run out of an inn, filled with anger, running towards a life alone, not thinking of anyone but himself. Now, his body pumping with anxiety, he ran head long into its opposite. His breath clawed in the cold, his feet pounding the stones, the effort jarring. He crossed the main street, dodging traffic, before turning down a slimmer lane that led into Honeysuckle Street. He sped past the duke's sandstone villa at Number 10, past the townhouses Number 9, Number 7, a curtain twitch at Number 5, past the ramshackle house, Abberton's, then the Hempel's at Number 3, the soprano's villa at Number 2, before finally rounding the corner of Babbage's at Number 1. The park came into view, and on the far side, beyond the frozen pond, a steeple sat stark against a weak blue sky. Sinclair strained his ears but could not hear church bells. If there were no bells, maybe he still had time.

Chapter Seventeen

In her one small rebellion against tradition, Charlise had insisted that she didn't need a maid of honour, or flower girls, but only her sister in her bridal ensemble. Elise's forest green dress set her eyes to verdant brilliance, and beside her, dressed in a lie of white lace, Charlise felt she might fade.

Pine boughs, cones, and red ribbons decorated the vestibule, and tapered candles flickered, their flames casting pin-sharp shadows of needles across the wall. Someone had stacked hymn books beside the collection plate, possibly in anticipation of the evening service when everyone would either come to church or be tucked up at home with their loved ones, trading gifts and singing around a piano.

Not tonight though. She would be on a train headed to Brighton. And a baroness.

The Hartright family usually sang on Christmas Eve, and she couldn't help but wonder how the little ensemble would sound without her. Since Mother passed, Father never joined in with much enthusiasm, and Aunt Petunia brought too much. Elise, wedged between them, would have to sing the melodies they normally shared.

'I wonder what the delay is. Perhaps he has gotten cold feet?' Elise said, a slight hope in her voice. Elise peeped into the church though a gap in the curtain. 'I know it's wrong to say this.' She spoke with an awkward hesitancy, as if debating continuing, then began to speak in a rush. 'But I feel I must. I do not like him. I wish you had chosen a different path. Being a woman with a reputation, it would not have haunted you forever.'

'I didn't choose this. I didn't have any choice.' Charlise folded back her veil. 'I'm not doing this for me. It's for you. To give you a chance to be your own person, free of my gossip and scandal. You must know, you are brilliant and beautiful and deserve every chance to shine.'

'For me?' A puzzled frown crossed Elise's face, and she shook her head. 'I don't believe you. You might think that, but ever since Mother died, you've been scared of everything. You don't want to be happy. You're like Father. You want to stay in your grief.'

Shuffling came from beyond the vestibule, followed by an uneven sound from the organ before a tune kicked into life.

'He's ready.' Father stepped into the little room. 'Charlise, your veil,' he muttered as he pulled it over her eyes again, sending the dullness of the room into a darker haze. She could barely tell the door to the church from the door to outside. This was why brides needed their fathers beside them. Not to give them support, but so they didn't walk the wrong way.

Elise paused at the vestibule, hovering. 'Be brave, Charlise,' she said, then took a steady step over the threshold, her long train trailing over the worn rug.

Charlise slipped her hand through her father's arm, counting off the rhythm of the march. Her father stepped out half a beat early, and she had to take two quick steps to match his pace.

'What was the delay?' she asked as they moved slowly past the congregation.

'Your husband wanted to settle some paperwork. We were just finalising an agreement over that house.'

'He's not my husband,' she sniped. 'Not yet.'

'He is as good as. Just a few words from you and it's settled. This whole sorry business will be over.'

Her next step was a little smaller. The one after, smaller again. What would be over? Their grief? Their family? So many things seemed about to end once she reached the altar that she couldn't be sure what he meant, because even she herself seemed about to end, and so completely that she'd no longer even have a name she recognised as her own.

Baroness Thistledown.

It didn't rhyme with Elise.

It didn't rhyme with anything.

'Father, I don't want to marry him.' She gripped his elbow, missing the next step in the march. 'And I don't want to be sorry anymore.'

'It's a bit late,' he gritted, a slight tussle in his next step. 'Love will grow. You'll see.'

'Please, Father. He is not a good man.'

'Charlise, everyone is watching,' her father hissed.

At the altar, the baron turned towards them, his head to one side. The congregation murmured, then shout cut through the hum of tense mutters.

'Charlise!' The door banged open, and Sinclair stomped indelicately into the church. A thin line of light surrounded his frame, all hard muscle and rough edges. His old suit was covered in dust, and he looked shabbier than she'd ever seen him. He extended his hand.

Charlise looked to her father, to the baron, the priest, and everyone, every thump in her chest ringing hard in her ears. The guests in the front row looked back. Her aunt, some cousins, a few people they'd recently met, all their eyes bored into her. Everyone watching, everyone waiting, and she wanted to wilt into submission. But then, she found Elise, and the world stilled. No one else mattered, not even Sinclair. Elise's bright green eyes reflected understanding, seeing everything there was to see, not just now, but the days, and weeks, and possibly years to follow.

'Go.' Her sister's voice didn't carry through the mutters of the church, but Charlise followed the shape of the word on her lips, read it in her eyes, and felt it in her heart. 'Be brave.'

Her father's grip slackened as he turned in confusion, and Charlise slipped her hand free of his crook, bunched her dress into her fist, and turned her back on the altar, the baron, on everything, and ran for the door. Her gloved hand clasped Sinclair's, and he laughed, bright and cracking, then tugged her through the vestibule and down the stairs, racing into the street.

'Where are we going,' she called, her voice already lighter than she'd heard it in years. Even with the shouts coming from behind, she felt unfettered, like the promise of freedom would give her the energy of a thousand childhoods running through grass and fields, and enough stamina to follow him anywhere.

'We are running away,' he shouted. 'Both of us.'

Somewhere by Hyde Park, they veered towards the river, streaking past shops and shoppers, dodging dogs and horses. The shops morphed to warehouses, pain bit beneath her lungs, her boots rubbed at her heels, and her breath came in gasps, until finally, along the docks, Sinclair slowed as he read the names painted on ship hulls, before finally giving a small leap and tugging her along the wharf.

'Permission to come aboard,' he called, waving his cap at a grey man leaning against the rail. 'That berth still available?'

'What in the name of Neptune?' The man replied, his eyes wide as he swept over the bulk of her dress, and before Charlise could take in the height of the masts and their thick white sails, Sinclair had tugged her up the gangplank. Once on deck, he pulled her to his chest, gripped her by the chin, and kissed her hard, his chest still heaving. At first, she returned his embrace, but as his hands flexed against the tight satin of her dress, and as the sweat that had dampened her bodice cooled, she shivered, then pulled back, her hand covering her mouth.

'What have I done? I was meant to make everything better.' Fear, her familiar friend, cloyed as the shocked looks of the congregation flashed before her. She looked to Sinclair, a face she adored, but also one she barely knew. 'I've only known you a week.' She clutched for the mast, a rope, for anything to stop her crumpling. Realisation crashed, its weight suffocating, and this time, she let it bear her down, choking sobs clawing, her breath still too puffed to properly release them. Silk, lace, and feathers puffed around her as she sunk to the deck and buried herself in their mass.

'Charlise.' Sinclair knelt beside her, his voice only a little louder than a whisper. 'Do you want me to take you back to the chapel?'

She stayed burrowed. She could claim nerves, vapours, or any number of excuses. The baron would take her back. He'd likely relish a new way to squeeze more money from her father, to hold her reputation to ransom a little longer. People would mutter, but so many already did. Everything would, approximately, be as it had been.

Be brave.

She inhaled hard, her breath tight in her chest. Swallowed, then exhaled, forcing air between her pursed lips. 'I can't marry him,' she blubbed. 'I just can't, but I—'

'Shh.' Sinclair wrapped his arm around her shoulder and pulled her against his chest. 'You don't have to marry him if you don't want to. Right now, you only have to do one thing, and that's breathe.'

All the fight went out of her as she slumped against him, took a shuddered breath, and then exhaled with a snuffled wail followed by tears.

CHAPTER EIGHTEEN

Sinclair tapped on the cabin door, swaying a little with the movement of the ship. He held a tray with tea, toast, and a thin sliver of fruit cake. It wasn't much as far as Christmas breakfasts went, but perhaps it would make her day feel a little more festive.

In the church, when Charlise had run to him and took his hand, he'd felt so certain that he was doing the right thing. But last night she'd cried so hard he didn't know how she hadn't shrivelled like an autumn leaf.

A murmured reply came from the other side of the door, and he levered it open, resting the tray against his waist as he squeezed through.

She had draped her wedding gown over a chair, and her stockings, corset, and petticoats sat folded on the desk. The delicate lace trimming and soft white cotton of her chemise blended with the sheets, and as he came in, she pulled them higher. Her skin looked as pale as the linen.

'I've brought tea. And toast.' He set the tray on the desk, then sat on the end of the bed beside the little mound of her feet. Drawn and exhausted, her dark hair ruffled and hanging scraggly, all he wanted to do was kiss her and tell her everything would be well. But he couldn't do that because he didn't even know it for himself.

'Where are we going?' she asked.

'Friedrich sails the clipper route. Fastest route between London and Australia. Down the Atlantic, and through the Roaring Forties, before landing in Melbourne.'

'You're going home?'

He nodded. 'Not sure I'll stay. Like Friedrich says, it's a big world, and I wouldn't mind seeing it. But I need to make my peace with my dad, and my family. It's a long journey, and not for the faint of heart.' He rested his hand on her feet, buried beneath the blankets. 'He'll make port at Plymouth and other stops along the way. You can go ashore anywhere you like. I've got enough coin to get you started, and I'd wager we could sell your dress for a good price. But if you'd like to make the journey to Melbourne with me, well, I've been thinking.' Sinclair shuffled up the bed and took up her hand, entwining his fingers with hers. Ever so faintly, she squeezed him back. 'Would you allow me to court you? I know it might feel a little awkward, given that we've already... And I must confess, all I want to do right now is throw you back against the pillows and love you all over again.' His eyes trailed down her neck to the gorgeous swell of her breasts, and with a wrench, he dragged his gaze back to her face. 'But you're a lady who deserves to be courted. Not negotiated. I've never much thought about courting anyone before, but I would very much like to court you.'

She stayed hunched, her body a ball.

'Friedrich has even offered to be your chaperone,' he continued, taking something from her silence. She had, after all, not rebuked him. 'Although, I'm not sure I'd trust him if it were my sister he was supervising, as he's also offered to be a look out if we'd like to break with propriety.'

She smiled, just a little, like she was trying on happiness to see if it fit. Then her teeth showed, and a small, optimistic giggle slipped out. 'I would like that,' she said, tucking her sheet closer, and higher, but something about the movement spoke of comfort and self-assuredness rather than fear.

'I should warn you, there isn't much more to me beyond what you've seen. But I feel you haven't had much joy, or choice, in your life of late. I can't give you much for Christmas, but I can give you that.'

He busied himself at setting her breakfast on the small desk, before making for the door with the tray. He'd be needed on deck soon.

'Sinclair?'

'Yes?' he spun around, bracing himself.

'Would Friedrich be so strict that he would not allow me a Christmas kiss?' And with that shy innocence he adored, she closed her eyes and raised her chin.

'I can't imagine he'd take much offence,' Sinclair said as he crossed the room, then bent to press his mouth to hers. There was nothing scandalous about it. Just the faintest brush of lips on lips, but as they touched, he felt as if every weight of his life had been concentrated.

Peace, beauty, and comfort.

Fear beyond anything he had ever known before.

And he knew that no matter what lay ahead, he would never be his own man because, always, there would be her.

He rested his forehead against hers. 'Merry Christmas, Miss Hartright,' he said, then stepped back towards the door. 'I am busy 'til nightfall. But this evening, would you like to take a turn around the decks?'

She nodded, and he knew he grinned like an idiot but didn't care. Just before he closed the door behind him, she called him back.

'Sinclair?'

He poked his head through the gap.

'Thank you,' she said as she pulled her tea into her lap. 'And Merry Christmas.'

CHAPTER NINETEEN

Later, back on Honeysuckle Street...
  17 May, 1871

Elise sat perched on the window seat in her aunt's front parlour, watching the workers across the street at Number 6. Today, they'd been trying to fix one of the side walls, but the frame had crumbled beneath the weight of the ladders. Miraculously, no one had been hurt.

And as usual, her father stood in front of the house, arguing with the baron. She was so familiar with their almost daily bickering that she could follow the conversation through their actions alone.

The baron flung his hands in the air. *I kept my word. I was at the church.*

Her father pointed at Aunt Petunia's as if he was thrusting his finger against her chest. *I have another daughter to launch. Her sister was supposed to sponsor her. What do I do now?*

The baron turned away, then back, and spread his arms. *Everyone is laughing at me. I need to show them I am not a man to be trifled with!*

Her father rubbed his temples. *I don't have the funds to mend your pride.*

Grief was a strange thing. When her mother had passed, all she could remember was feeling so deeply sad that she had gone, but also relieved that she was no longer in pain. The contrary feelings never melded, but only battered against each other. And Elise felt that same squall now. So happy that her sister wasn't married to the awful man who stood prodding her father in the chest, but also missing her with a ferocity that sometimes made her joints ache and woke her at night where she would lie helpless, staring across at the empty bed by the window, weeping.

A brisk knock sounded, and Elise leant out as her aunt's butler answered the door and showed in Miss Abberton, dressed in travelling clothes. She held a thick, cream envelope in her hand, and as she crossed the room, she held it out to Elise.

'Papa received a delivery,' she said as she took up a seat beside the window. 'A crate of cordial syrup. And this envelope was inside. We have only just returned from our travels, so I have no idea how long it has been sitting there, but I brought it over straight away.'

She should have been trembling, but as Elise took the envelope, she stayed steady. A familiar hand had penned her name across the parchment. Elise cracked the gum paste seal, took out the thick cream letter, and unfolded it. Once she'd absorbed the contents, she rose and gave Miss Abberton a nod, then walked out onto the street to find her father.

'She may come back,' the baron said, another pleading line in the daily play between the two men who had seen her sister's ruination as a problem to be erased or exploited, and not the cry of a grieving daughter needing compassion.

Elise held out the letter. 'Father. She's not coming back.'

The two of them turned towards her almost in unison, both of them blinking as if seeing her for the first time. Then her father snatched the letter, his eyes darting across the page, before his expression turned black.

If only she had read it more than once. Or torn the corner with the address and stuffed it in her pocket before handing it over. But she hadn't. Her father's eyes raced over the lines, then he cursed and grasped the letter before tearing it in two, then he turned it and ripped it again. Even though Elise cried out for him to stop, he continued shredding her sister's words, then threw all the small pieces into the air. She grasped helplessly as each sliver caught a summer breeze and flew higher, before fanning out across the city. She chased them, clutching for random fragments, before she realised it would be pointless. Her sister was gone. She watched the slips and imagined them twisting into wholeness again, and as they flittered out of reach, she cemented in her memory as much of the note as she could, before watching it fly away.

My darling, my beautiful Elise,

How many times have I put pen to paper, and then overwhelmed with grief and fear, have put it aside. How many times have I been terrified of what reply I might receive, and so decided not to write. But today, I have found courage.

Do you remember when you asked me if I imagined courting could be magic? As we have sailed from one side of the world to the other, from the top to the bottom, how often have I thought of that conversation, and I want you to know that I have known magic! When we landed in Cape Hope, and Sinclair escorted me along the pier, not even begging a kiss. When he held me through the most ferocious storm as we traversed the Atlantic. When, one evening, we lay on the deck, the ship completely still as we waited for a wind, with only our cheeks touching, staring up at the stars. All of it was magic.

What more can I say? I am married. Not in an elaborate ceremony in a well-to-do chapel, but on a ship's deck, and then, when we found that

Friedrich was simply bored with being my chaperone and not exactly empowered to conduct a wedding ceremony, again in a church on Collins Street once we made port.

Please write. If you forgive me, if you are happy for me, please, please write. The pain I feel when I think of you is indescribable. I miss you so intently, so completely, like a part of myself has been severed. Sary, Sinclair's sister, is delightful. His brothers are gruff, but also caring. They call him little, even though he is a foot over all of them! But none of them are you. Even Sinclair, who lights my days, the joy he brings cannot warm that space in my heart that misses you more than a buried crocus misses the sun.

Every beat of your heart, I am there.

Your sister, always,

Charlise.

The scattered link disappeared from her view, and in one moment, she both loved her sister more than anything in the world and despised her.

'Jonathan. Enough is enough.'

The street stilled as every workman, every pedestrian, the baron, even Mrs Crofts peeking through her curtains, all of them looked at Aunt Petunia as she stood before her brother and the baron.

'This is my solicitor, Mr Fitzherbert.' Aunt Petunia gestured at the tall man beside her who clutched his leather satchel. 'He has been reviewing your lordship's claim.'

'I read over your claim.' Mr Fitzherbert said, deliberate and officious. 'Other precedents, and the like. And, your advisers may disagree, but I am not certain the courts would side with you. They may agree to some compensation, but to settle funds as if the marriage had taken place? To hand over ownership of this house, complete with renovations?' He shook his head. 'Unlikely.'

'I will not be treated this way,' the baron said, his chest heaving. 'I am Baron Thistle—'

'We are all well aware of who you are,' Aunt Petunia stepped forward. 'You are the nobleman who was jilted for a common cordial maker. We also know that you have abandoned your mistress in Soho, even though she is carrying your child, and that you have a brother who seduced his wife's cousin, and both of you have unpaid debts all over town. Shall I continue? Or will you agree to leave this street and return to your estate.' Aunt Petunia's voice dropped. 'What remains of it anyway.'

'How did you—' the baron spluttered, looking fast between everyone.

'As you said, your lordship, many of my neighbours are esteemed men. Some of them are dukes. Others have exemplary connections.'

In her periphery, Elise noted the baron stalk off, climb into his sulky, and then bark some command at his horse before being driving away. And while relief at his departure blew through her, it seemed only a background to her father, who now knelt on the road, a few scraps of paper scattered around him.

'Jonathan,' Aunt Petunia stepped closer. 'You have a daughter who needs you. Come inside.'

He stayed hunched, like a wounded beast, his form rising and falling with heavy breaths. 'Tear it down,' he muttered, before leaping to his feet with an anguished shout and striding to the front of Number 6. 'Do you hear me?' he shouted at the workers, his arms waving. 'Tear the whole bloody thing down!'

Perhaps craving a release from the danger they faced each day in trying to repair an unfixable house, or relieved to be free of the daily bickering, or perhaps in a rush to escape her father's ranting, all the workmen moved into action. Hauling brick, raising ladders, and chipping away at easily fragmenting walls, workers swarmed until the tilting frame of Number 6 leaned, then began to crumble under its own weight.

'What are they doing?' Elise had forgotten about Miss Abberton, who now raced down her aunt's stairs and across the street to join them. 'Why are they tearing down Number 6? They can't, it's where we used to... it's where...'

But what the house meant to Iris, she didn't say, only pulled Elise against her side and wiped her cheeks with her handkerchief. And as the labourers worked, the three of them stood shoulder to shoulder, hands gripped as they watched each brick fall, the wooden frame crumble, and the doors clap flat against the ground as the glass shrieked. And from the wreckage, Spencer, the grey tom with a white-tipped tail, streaked from behind a set of stairs before they collapsed. Elise scooped him into her arms and nuzzled into the comfort of his soft fur.

'I need a drink,' Aunt Petunia announced. 'Something a little stronger than syrup. I think brandy is in order. Ladies?'

Elise stroked Spencer's fur, then turned to follow her aunt.

'You. You knew. At the church, you told her to run.' Her father pushed himself to his feet before pointing at her aunt's house. 'Pack your trunk.'

Elise loved her sister ferociously. Loved her kindness and her compassion. But she had always been in the shadow of her beauty and her voice. For the first time in her life, she felt herself standing in her father's total gaze, and she decided that it was not where she wanted to be.

And if her sister could be brave, then so could she.

'No,' she said, the determination in her heart not reaching her voice. 'I think I would like to stay a little longer with Aunt Petunia.'

And without waiting for his reply, Elise burrowed her tears in Spencer's fur and ascended the stairs to Number 7, following her aunt and Iris, before pushing the door closed behind her.

Historical Notes

Honeysuckle Street is not a real London street.

It is based on the very real changes that were taking place across town planning at the time, where older style, freestanding villas were gradually being knocked down and replaced with townhouses, usually build to a single plan. This style of townhouse is ubiquitous in London, and many other major cities, who with changes in knowledge about germs, ideas about class division and the rise of the middle class had a massive influence on physical spaces and places. This is the world that Honeysuckle Street lives in—a world in flux, living with the old but with eyes firmly fixed on the new.

In Chapter Three, the lines Charlise sings are from *See Amid the Winter's Snow*, also known as *The Hymn for Christmas*, written by Edward Caswall and first published in 1858.

Sinclair refers to *The Handbook of Etiquette: Being a Complete Guide to the Usages of Polite Society*, first published in 1860. It was one of the many etiquette guides available at the time, designed to help the newly wealthy navigate the complex social hierarchy and rules of Victorian society.

ALSO BY AND FORTHCOMING

Tales from Honeysuckle Street

A Beginner's Guide to Scandal

A Most Improper Duchess

Forthcoming

Undercover with the Heiress – *November 2024*

Blueprints, Battlelines and Ballrooms

Last Song for the Soprano

All is Fair in Love and Diplomacy

For Elise

Heartbeats of History – Steamy Short Stories

Tryst with a Viscount

The Portrait Sitting

Hide and Seek

My Fake Mistress

About Alivia

Hi! My name is Alivia, and I write steamy romance for history lovers.

I started writing romance in 2022. At first I wanted to write short stories, but then my characters kept turning up with copious amounts of back story, demanding I help them solve their problems! In April, 2023, I published my first novel, *A Beginner's Guide to Scandal,* the first in my series, Tales from Honeysuckle Street.

My novella, *The Portrait Sitting*, is a Romance Writers of Australia RUBY award winning story.

I live on a farm a long way from anywhere interesting, with my husband, our three dogs, and a charismatic chicken named Persephone.

You can learn more about me, my stories and upcoming releases at aliviafleur.com

www.ingramcontent.com/pod-product-compliance
Lightning Source LLC
Chambersburg PA
CBHW030233180626
46810CB00008B/3109